Also by

Shannon Esposito

SAHARA'S SONG

STRANGE NEW FEET

THE MONARCH

KARMA'S A BITCH

Lady Luck Runs Out

(A Pet Psychic Mystery No. 2)

A NOVEL

Shannon Esposito

misterio press

Lady Luck Runs Out

(A Pet Psychic Mystery No. 2)

Copyright © Shannon Esposito, 2012
Published by misterio press

Printed in The United States of America

* * * * *

Visit Shannon Esposito's official website at
www.murderinparadise.com

* * * * *

Cover Art by India Drummond

Formatting by Debora Lewis
arenapublishing.org

* * * * *

ISBN-13: 978-1482336894

Dedicated to my family
for their endless support.

PROLOGUE

Rose Faraday knew it was time to stop ignoring her niggling gut and the metaphorical neon-flashing signs the universe had been manifesting around her. She lowered herself onto the sofa, unwrapped her tarot cards from their silk fabric covering and spread the cloth out on the coffee table. A long-haired, black cat wound itself around her ankle, and then deposited a fake mouse on her foot. "Mew!"

She smiled down into eyes as green and clear as emeralds and sighed. "Not now, Lucky, Mama's got to work." She scratched the cat under the belly with her bare toes and then pushed her gently away, "Go on, we'll play fetch later. Scooch." Lucky squeaked out one more "mew" in protest then sauntered off, hopping through the cat door to the screened lanai, where her favorite scratching post awaited.

Rose took a deep breath, letting the scent of the burning jasmine incense relax her, and closed her eyes. When she felt ready, she opened and took out the time-softened cards, arranging them in three piles on the silk. The mounting feeling of dread had prompted her to read for herself today and she needed to be relaxed. To concentrate on the question: Am I in physical danger?

After shuffling the cards three times, she slid the first one off the pile and laid it down. Ten of Swords. Her least favorite card. Well, things couldn't get worse, that wasn't exactly bad news. She slid the next card off the deck and placed it upright to the left of the Ten of Swords.

The Death Card. Rose stared at the skeletal face in the black armor. So, something was coming to an end? A transformation? She held the question "Am I in physical danger?" in the forefront of her mind. Heaviness fell upon her. She shivered. Then again, sometimes death just meant death.

Rose shook off the thought and pulled a third card, placing it to the right of the Ten of Swords. Judgment reversed. She noted her own reaction to this card, a nervousness that she knew meant the card wasn't just about closing a door on the past and having a new beginning. It was about a decided end.

Defiantly, she pulled a fourth clarifying card and placed it to the right of Judgment.

The Six of Swords. She always subscribed to the belief this card represented Charon, the ferryman who shuttled the departed across the River Styx. With all the other cards preceding this one, it was hard to ignore the possibility she was indeed in physical danger. Her breath grew shallow and she had to force herself to deepen it, to calm her thoughts. Her left hand fluttered to the gold cuff bracelet on her right wrist and began twisting it, as was her habit when she felt anxious. It had been her mother's. The one piece of jewelry that hadn't been buried with her.

Okay. One more clarifying card.

Rose flipped it over and placed it to the left of the Death card.

The Devil. Another dark card. She involuntarily pushed back away from the spread in front of her. Fear wound its way through her body, causing the hair on the back of her neck to prickle. She wiped the sweat from her upper lip.

A crash from the lanai made her jump. She placed a hand on her racing heart. Good gracious! Sounded like Lucky knocked over one of her potted plants again.

"Lucky, leave the lizards alone!" she called. That cat would never learn. She'd deal with the mess later. Right now she had more important things to worry about.

Rose gathered up the cards and wrapped them back up. It was time to consult her crystal ball. With trembling hands, she retrieved it and set it on the coffee table in front of her.

Rose took a few deep breaths to let the turmoil of anxiety sink to the bottom and let her mind clear. Then she began to rub the crystal ball. Its cool surface gave her comfort. Scrying had always been one of her strongest gifts, one of the few useful things her mother had passed down to her.

When she felt calmer and focused, she opened her eyes and stared into the quartz ball, watching light flutter around in its fractured depths. Seconds ticked by, then minutes unnoticed as she continued to hold her focus. A gray mist began to form, swirling and darkening until a black storm raged within the confines of the sphere. Rose's heart fluttered nervously. This was not going to be good news. She visualized the storm disintegrating and watched as the inky, cloudy ball became clear once again.

A serpent sat, coiled tightly, its eyes shifting from black to red. A chill traveled up Rose's arms. She pulled her hands away as if the ball had caught fire.

One hand still resting protectively over her heart, she mulled over the image.

Okay, snakes and their shedding skin symbolize change, releasing old habits. That's what the Devil card must be telling her. She just needed to let go of an old habit. She twisted the bracelet roughly around her arm. Well, crap, she was going to have to give up her pack a day smoking habit. Sure, that made sense. After all, she was fifty-three and had a congenital heart defect, probably pushing her luck, anyway. Didn't take a crystal ball to figure that out.

But, the panic wasn't receding. No matter how she tried to justify the cards and the serpent vision, no matter how hard she tried to push them to the corners of her mind, anxiety fluttered in every cell of her body.

Smoothing out her creased skirt, she nodded. Okay, time to take a break and see what kind of mess her beloved girl made this time. Besides, she could use a quick cuddle. Hearing Lucky's motorboat purr always calmed her nerves.

Rose stood up and took one step. Her right bare foot came down on something cold and hard. She glanced down just in time to register the diamond pattern before a quick strike sent venom coursing through her leg. She squealed, confused, as the diamond back rattler's tail disappeared beneath her sofa. Searing heat radiated up her leg and she fell over onto the sofa, clutching her heart. White hot pain blossomed in her chest, squeezing the breath out of her. She gasped for air.

So, this was it? A literal snake?! Images flashed through her mind. The Devil card grew larger, until she could see the scales on his face, see herself reflected in his beady black eyes. His tongue flicked out at her. She felt so cold. The pain in her chest was unbearable. Her last thought was of her cat. "Lucky, run!"

CHAPTER ONE

I gasped as I opened a box of handmade quilted waterproof dog coats. "Oh, aren't these just gorgeous!" From where I was kneeling behind the counter, I held up a tiny tangerine-colored one.

"Stephanie is *muita talentoso*!" Sylvia pulled up her daily schedule on the computer with one hand, an apple turnover in the other.

I swear, I don't know how that woman keeps her figure. She lives on baked goods.

"Mrs. Janicki is first today with Barbie, the little Chiweenie. Barbie needs a coat, poor bebê, she just shakes all the time."

"Probably more nerves than cold." I grinned up at Sylvia. "She's probably afraid someone's going to make fun of her for being a Chiweenie." Such funny names they give these designer dogs. "Grab some Aspen and Cherry Plum flower essence before you groom her. Should help calm her down."

"Okay." Sylvia slipped her white lab coat over a turquoise dress, flipping her dark, silky ponytail from the collar. "Three drops?"

"Yeah, that should be fine."

I smiled to myself as Sylvia walked back to the store room, licking the last of the pastry off her fingers. I had to give her credit. It had only been five months since we opened Darwin's Pet Boutique together and she'd gone from laughing at my flower essence as "woo woo" stuff to actually using it on her clients. Maybe there was hope yet for me being able to confide in her about my family secrets.

After I hung up the new coats and restocked the fortune cookie boxes on the doggie treat table, I checked the clock on the wall. Ten minutes until opening time. Plenty of time for a second cup of tea.

I glanced out the window as I poured hot water into my glass mug. The sidewalks were already beginning to fill up with people enjoying the clear October Florida morning. I was learning that fall in St. Pete was a whole different animal than summer. At least here in our little strip of paradise on Beach Drive. Here the brisker air turned lazy summer days into days people spent shopping, exploring and chatting in a myriad of colorful world accents.

Shaking some Ginseng Oolong tea leaves into the mesh infuser, I watched a taxi pull up, my mind already on the tasks for the day. First thing this morning I needed to call around and see if I could find a life jacket big enough for Gillian Smith's Great Dane. I wasn't sure where they were going to find a boat big enough, I chuckled to myself. That dog was as sweet as pie but big as a horse. Then I needed to order—

Suddenly, my mouth dropped open. "Holy heaven on a stick!" I squealed.

"Darwin?" Sylvia hustled from the back, her heels clicking on the wood floor. "*What é errado?*" She stood beside me, catching her breath, peering outside and trying to figure out what had me standing there gawking. "What is it?"

I lifted a finger to point at the red head gathering her bags from the taxi. "It... it's my baby sister."

"Really?" Sylvia cocked her head and folded her arms. "Huh. She looks nothing like you. She is the youngest one, no? The eighteen year old? Very pretty."

I turned to Sylvia, but I didn't see her. I was still reeling from shock, working out all the implications of Mallory's presence here. *Was someone dying? Was she here to talk me into going home?* I hadn't spoken to my Mom or two sisters since I moved to St. Pete five months ago. Not by choice, they just didn't understand or appreciate me "abandoning" them. *Does this mean I was forgiven?*

A curious smile tugged at Sylvia's perfectly glossed lips. "You should unlock the door."

"Right." By the time I retrieved the keys and unlocked the door, Mallory was waving to me from the other side. I pushed it open and tried to shove aside all the questions and just be happy she was there. "Hey, Mal! You're here... in St. Pete. I can't believe it!"

Mallory's eyes glittered mischievously as she gave me a stiff hug. "Yep. I'm here."

I reached down and helped her bring in her bags and guitar case as she glanced around the boutique. "You've decided to be around pets? In the place you're trying to make a new start?" She turned and stared at me. "Now that's interesting."

Sylvia glanced from me to Mallory and held out her hand. "*Olá*. I'm Sylvia, Darwin's business partner."

Mallory shook her hand. "Hi, I'm Mallory, Darwin's sister. Did you know she has two sisters?"

Sylvia glanced at me and smirked. Yeah, she knew that was a dig at me. "Of course. Darwin, she talks about you and Willow all the time. It's nice to meet you in person."

"She does?" Mallory glanced back at me, her eyes narrowing.

Just then the door bell jingled behind me and Mrs. Janicki strolled in carrying Barbie in a pink Betty Boop designer bag that matched her pink running suit. "Good morning, ladies."

"Good morning, Mrs. Janicki." Sylvia bent down to Barbie's level and gently stroked her head. "And how's our *pequena* this morning?"

"Excited and ready for her makeover." Mrs. Janicki fluffed her newly bleached and rolled hair. "Can we use the lavender shampoo today?"

"Of course." Sylvia turned. "It was nice to meet you, Mallory." Then she began chatting with Mrs. Janicki as she led her back to the grooming room.

"What was that thing? A rat?" Mallory stared after them. "Poor thing was shaking like a leaf."

"A Chiweenie," I said, moving to the counter.

"A Chi... what?"

"Never mind." I straightened out the pamphlets on the counter, glancing at my sister. "So, what brings you here, Mal?" I noted the irritation in her eyes as she turned them on me. I put more enthusiasm in my tone. "I mean, I'm happy as a puppy with two tails to see you. I'm just surprised, that's all. How long are you staying?"

She shrugged and leaned down to scope out the dog treats in the glass case. "You make these?"

"Yes." Now I was getting irritated. She always was good at evading questioning.

"Cool." She straightened up and sighed. "Mom thought it would be a good idea to send me here and make sure you were okay since we hadn't heard from you." She folded her arms. "And plus, you left a few things behind we thought you might need."

I saw the gold sparks flash in her green eyes. Yeah, she was still angry with me for leaving. I forced a smile. What I had left behind, I left behind on purpose. But, I wasn't going to get into that discussion with her right now. "Thanks. That was thoughtful." Also, I wasn't going to get into the fact that I wasn't the one not returning calls.

Customers began to trickle through the door. After I greeted them, I gave Mallory my gate card to the townhouse above the boutique and instructions on how to get to it. I was renting the two story "city home" from Sylvia, who purchased it with her grandfather's inheritance money. The oversized million dollar place was a bit overkill for one person, but I couldn't beat the location. "Go put your bags away and make yourself at home. I'll come up and take you to lunch around one o'clock, okay?" I gave her a hug. "It really is good to see you."

CHAPTER TWO

I came home to find the leather bound books and chalice I had left behind in Savannah staring accusingly at me from the kitchen bar. Perfect. I decided to just ignore them for now.

"Mallory?" Her bags were still by the door. "Where are you?"

"Out here."

Moving into the living room, I saw the French doors were wide open. I found her in a peach bikini top and shorts, recharging her batteries on the balcony. She gets energy from the sun like I get it from water. Her guitar sat at her feet. My heart ached at the common sight, and I realized how much I had missed her. How much I missed my family and all their idiosyncrasies.

"Ready for lunch?"

"Yep." She slipped a t-shirt on over her bikini top. "Just soakin' in some of this delicious Florida sunshine. Is it always this nice in October?"

"Not sure." I shrugged. This was my first fall in Florida, but she knew that. I wasn't about to remind her. "This is going to have to be a short lunch. The boutique is slammed today so I can't be gone long. Sylvia's holding down the fort but her next appointment will be there in half an hour." I led her back down the elevator, through the garden gate and out to the busy Beach Drive sidewalk. "We'll just hop over to Hooker Tea Company. They have quick service."

A young couple was just getting up from the table outside that held a special place in my heart. I snagged it and sat Mallory down. "Wait here. I'll get us lunch."

I emerged ten minutes later with sandwiches and iced tea. "Here we go." Sliding into the seat under the umbrella, I felt her staring at me over her food.

"So," she said. "Is being away from us all that you thought it would be?"

Ouch. And so the jabs begin. I glanced up at her as she bit into her tuna sandwich.

"That's not fair, Mallory. You know I didn't leave to be away from you or Willow or Mom. I just wanted a fresh start, where nobody knows our family." I mentally smacked myself. I knew when I said it she would take it wrong, oh she-of-quick-temper. I wasn't disappointed.

Her eyes blazed. "So, you're ashamed of us?"

I took a bite of my red pepper and hummus sandwich and counted to ten. I could have reminded her of the disastrous eighth grade sleepover or the hurtful article that appeared in our local paper after a reporter took Willow out on a ruse date. What's not to be ashamed of? Instead I swallowed and said, "You know that's not what I meant. I just want to be able to make friends without wondering what their motivations are or wondering what they've heard about us."

She sipped the iced tea and leaned back. "So, have you... made friends?"

My heart squeezed. "Yeah, I have."

Her brow shot up. "Friends that don't know the real you?"

Heavens, she knew how to hit where it hurt. I silently took another bite and swallowed the lump in my throat with it. No way to answer that. She was right.

"Sylvia seems nice." She picked at some lettuce, her tone softening. "Have you made any guy friends?"

I nodded and decided to tell her about Mad Dog. I wasn't ready to tell her about Will. I felt protective of him and didn't want her opinion of our relationship. "The first friend I had when I moved here was a homeless guy named Mad Dog." I watched her pause midway through a sip of tea. Holding up a hand I continued, "I know what you're thinking, but he was a good guy. Had a good heart. Just a rough life. Unfortunately, he was killed." Mallory sat back in her chair and stared at me, wide-eyed. I kept going. "He had this big sweet, slobbery lug of a mastiff named Karma. Long story short, Karma helped me... you know, find out who killed Mad Dog." I whispered this last part.

"He was murdered? So, you've been here a few months and already solved a murder?" Her eyes now lit up with the excitement of adventure. "I can't wait to hear this story."

I checked my watch. "It'll have to wait until later. Five minute warning."

Disappointed, Mallory bit into her sandwich and picked up a flyer that was left on the table. "Hey, let's do this tonight!"

I chewed as I read the flyer. "A ghost tour?"

"Yeah, it'll be fun."

I shrugged. "All right. If that's what you want to do. How long are you staying anyway?" I figured eventually I'd get an answer to that question.

Something flashed in her eyes. Worry? Fear? "Until I buy a return ticket home."

Fabulous.

CHAPTER THREE

Around eight o'clock that night we joined a group of about a dozen other ghost seekers inside Hooker Tea Company. Heavens, it smelled good in there; sweet and spicy with undercurrents of ginger, peaches, peppermint and jasmine. Someone walked by with a cup of fresh mango black. That was it. I had to order a cup.

"You want something?" I asked Mallory.

She took a seat in one of their paisley armchairs. "Whatever you're having."

Our guide came in while we were happily sipping our tea and chatting with a couple from Canada. The guide was a woman in her fifties, dressed in black and carrying a lantern. She had warm brown eyes and a calm spirit. I liked her immediately. She introduced herself as Mary.

"Welcome, everyone! It's a gorgeous night for spotting ghosts." After she urged us all to introduce ourselves and say where we were from, she smiled. "Okay, let's go ahead and get started."

The traffic broke for us as we followed Mary and her lantern across the street to North Straub Park. The park trees sparkled with white lights strung through their branches. The Vinoy Resort lit up the far edge of the park to the north. The air held the scent of the Bay waters. I soaked it all in.

Everyone crowded around Mary in the muted darkness as she rattled off a few ghost stories about the area and encouraged us to snap random pictures.

"You never know what... or who... you'll capture."

It was a star-filled, clear night and had only dropped down to the mid sixties. Still, I pulled my sweater tighter around me and smiled as I watched Mallory eagerly snap photos with her phone. It really was good to see her. I had missed her particular brand of enthusiasm. It was contagious.

"Hey, my camera froze up!" A petite lady, who had introduced herself earlier as Bobbie from Michigan, said excitedly.

"That happens a lot." Mary nodded knowingly. "The theory is the spirits drain the energy from our batteries and electronics to use for things like manifesting and communicating. Look back through your photos. Anyone catch anything?"

"Look at this, I think I got somethin'!" Brynn, a coltish teenage girl with a pixie cut, called out. Everyone migrated toward her on the lawn, taking turns peering at her phone screen.

"Looks like an orb," Bobbie exclaimed.

Mallory took her turn and shrugged. "Looks like dust to me."

"All right, time to move on to our next spot." Mary led us back across Beach Drive, down a dark sidewalk, to a gray house that had been worn from the elements and time. Boards crisscrossed the bottom floor windows but the second story sported curtains. I strained through the darkness for any sign of fluttering or movement. Mallory held her phone up and snapped a couple photos. We took turns peering in the front porch windows and listening to the story of the woman who died there, apparently a murder that went unsolved. More photos. More orbs. Mallory shifted beside me, messing with the tendrils of hair on her neck that had escaped her hair tie. She was getting antsy.

Our next stop was the Traveler's Palm Inn: a lime-green hotel, built in the fifties and rumored to be haunted by three male ghosts who had died violently there. We all filed into the conference room on the bottom floor.

Mary moved to the side of the door. "Now be warned, we've had women get their hair and clothes tugged on in here. We're going to go ahead and turn the lights off. We seem to get more activity that way."

A flick of Mary's hand threw the room into semi-darkness. The left wall held three windows that let in enough moonlight to see shadows and shapes. Short bursts of flash began to occur as people ventured deeper into the conference room.

After a few minutes, a voice broke the silence. "I saw something in the corner over there! A shadow."

"Oh please," Mallory whispered beside me. "Shadows, orbs, blah, blah, blah." I turned to her, planning on telling her not to ruin these people's fun but she had no intention of doing that. In fact, she planned on enhancing their ghost busting experience.

I wasn't sure what she was doing at first and then, as a motorcycle passed by the window and lit us enough for me to see her hands working, I grabbed her arm. "No, Mal!"

But it was too late. A tiny ball of energy shot from her palm and ping ponged around the room.

A few squeals and gasps precluded a frenzy of flashing as the ghost hunters tried to capture it on film.

"Everyone stay calm!" Mary called into the room. "Be mindful of the people around you."

Suddenly, a dark figure leapt from the shadows. A large black cat had apparently been startled from its hiding place by the flying orb.

It bound toward us and Mallory shrieked as it pounced on her, digging its claws into her back as it tried to balance on her shoulder. "Ow, ow! What in heaven...? Darwin, help!"

I grabbed the cat around its soft middle, intending to pry its claws gently from my sister's back, but as soon as my palms touched it, I got zapped. Hard.

Energy rushed through me like a tidal wave, flooding me with sounds, smells and a few clear images.

A shadow person dressed in a black jacket and hood, creeping up to a lanai screen in the dark. A horrible whiff of something dank and sour. A tearing sound. A hissing as a large snake slithered on the ground then, lifting its head, flicked its tongue right at me.

I fell back, releasing my grip on the cat and landing hard on my bottom.

"Darwin? You okay?" Mallory yelled over the other excited voices. The cat still clung stubbornly to her shoulder so she supported its butt with one hand to keep it from digging into her skin for leverage.

I pushed myself off the floor, trembling. Every cell in my body hummed as the energy surged through me, building in intensity until it settled into a steady throbbing behind my eyes.

Had... to... disperse... it.

"Fine." I pushed out between frantic jumping jacks. "Just saw..." I switched to running in place. "... something." My legs tingled like they had fallen asleep. Heat pulsed around my organs and through my blood. *Poor kitty. This was a bad one.*

Zing! I sagged in relief as the energy finally broke free from the confines of my body. My temperature began to drop back to normal. I began to shiver in the air-conditioned room.

Mary flicked on the lights. My eyes widened. Oh, good grief. The energy I had expelled headed straight for the orb.

It sought out the ball of light Mallory had created, joined it and expanded it like a balloon until it was the size of a car tire. People stopped taking pictures and started screaming, stumbling over each other trying to get out the door. Mallory and I scrambled to move out of the way so we didn't get knocked down.

Within a few seconds, we were the only ones left in the room. Mallory stood there in shock with the black cat still quivering and clinging to her. I stood beside her, trembling and going over the vision I had received from the traumatized cat.

I reached out and stroked the soft, black fur. Glowing eyes peered at me from beneath Mallory's hair. "You poor thing. It's all right, you're safe now."

We stayed in the room until the orb burned itself out, and then made our exit out into the hotel lobby. Our group was huddled by the front doors, comparing photos they had captured and chatting excitedly. Mary made her way over to us, her black cape askew, her face flushed.

"Are you gals okay?" She spotted the ball of fur clinging to Mallory. "Oh my! I see you found a stowaway."

"More like it found me." Mallory lightly patted the cat's rump above its flicking tail. Cats have always been attracted to Mallory. Luckily, the feeling was mutual.

"Looks well taken care of. I don't think it's a stray." I reached over and flipped the little metal tag over on its diamond studded collar. "Says her name's Lady Luck. There's an address." I glanced at Mary. "I hope you don't think us rude, but we're going to cut out of the ghost tour early, see if we can't return this girl back to her owner." In truth, I was feeling nervous. If that snake was in the house with the cat, it might still be in the house with the owner. Which meant the owner could be in danger.

"Not at all..." Mary assured us with a wave. "I'm sure somebody is worried sick about this pretty gal. Besides, I think that was about as much excitement as you're gonna get on a tour."

"Thanks." I smiled. We made our way through the knot of excited people and out onto the sidewalk. Mallory plugged the address into the map on her phone and we set off to find Lady Luck's owner.

We'd been walking in silence for about twenty minutes, being extra careful at each street crossing after we had witnessed a minor accident between two cars, both of which thought they had the right of way.

"Holy Moly, this girl is getting heavy," Mallory breathed, readjusting the mass of fur on her shoulder. "Maybe we should fetch a cab."

I checked the display on her phone. "We only have two blocks to go." I had already tried to take Lady Luck off my sister's hands, but she was having none of it. She just dug her claws in deeper.

"So, what did you see anyway?" Mallory huffed beside me.

The vision came back to me and my stomach clenched. "A snake."

"A snake? What kind of snake?"

"I don't know. A big one."

"Huh," Mallory responded. "So this cat had a run in with a snake? No wonder she's so freaked."

"Yeah, but that's not the worst part. I think her owner might be in danger. The run-in wasn't outdoors. Over there." I motioned across the street to the back lawn of a small golf course. "The condos are behind there, let's cut across."

We trekked over the soft terrain and rolling hills toward the row of lights indicating the back yards of Golf Gate Estates. Once there, we followed the GPS directions down one of the paved streets. Each gray stucco building held four condos with white trim and perfectly manicured bushes."Look for number 457. It should be here on the right somewhere."

"There." Mallory pointed with her chin.

It was an end unit. We approached the door and mashed the door bell. No answer. I knocked. We waited. I stared down at the cat. Her round glowing eyes stared back at me. She looked hopeful but I had a sinking feeling this wasn't going to be her lucky night. I knocked again, harder.

"Not home?"

I glanced at Mallory, my stomach tightening. *Not home or not able to answer the door?* "Come on, let's check around back. Stay behind me." I picked my way carefully through the thick, damp grass, watching for any sign of slithery movement. Alligator calls from the golf course lakes echoed through the night air. A few bat silhouettes fluttered in the sky above. Florida at nighttime seemed to be just as active as Florida in the daytime.

We reached the backyard without any reptile run-ins. The back of the condo units had attached screened lanais and this one had the porch light burning bright. I tugged at the door. Locked from the inside.

"Ow, ow, ow," Mallory whispered. I looked behind me to see the cat clawing its way back onto Mallory's shoulder to hide under her mass of red hair.

"That's not good," I whispered. "She can probably smell the snake if it's still here."

"The snake can probably smell her, too," Mallory shot back. "It was probably looking for a meal."

I walked the parameter of the lanai. A plant stand had been knocked over. A broken pot lay on the tile, its contents of dark dirt and pale plant strewn across the floor. I brought back the images from the vision. *How exactly did the snake get in and Lady Luck get out?* I crouched down and activated Malloy's phone, shining the light across the bottom of the screen. *There!* Crab walking to my right, I stuck my hand beneath the part of the screen at the bottom that was fluttering slightly in the breeze and lifted it. "Big enough for a cat to run out."

"So, she spotted the snake and tore through the screen?" Mallory asked.

I shook my head. "I think it was already torn open."

"By the snake?"

I ignored her sarcasm. "Something like that." *Maybe a snake of the human variety.*

This just didn't seem right. Lady Luck witnessed a man-sized shadow in front of the screen before the snake slithered in. Did that person cut the screen and let the snake in? Why would someone do that? I snapped a picture of the ripped screen. It was time to call Will. Using Mallory's cell phone, I dialed his number.

CHAPTER FOUR

The breeze held a chill. I was glad I had worn a sweater as we sat, huddled on the curb. Lucky seemed content in Mallory's lap but her whiskers and ears kept flicking nervously. I couldn't even imagine what the poor thing was thinking right now. So close to her home, yet she couldn't go in. Someone was grilling. The smell of charred beef wafted through the night air.

Will's sedan rolled around the circle, its headlights raking us before he pulled up and shut them off. I suddenly remembered I hadn't told Mallory about Will. Oops. Too late now.

We stood up as he approached. "Hey." He slipped his hand easily behind my neck and gave me a quick hello kiss. "What's going on?"

"Yeah, sis, what's going on?" Mallory's eyes narrowed as she adjusted Lucky in her arms and gave Will the once over.

Here we go. "Will." I held out my hand. "Meet my sister, Mallory. Mallory... Will."

They shook hands over the cat. Mallory shoved her tongue in her cheek. "And you are Darwin's—"

"Friend." I cut her off. Our relationship was awkward enough without my sister trying to define it. I had fallen for Will hard but had to slow things down or let him in on our family secrets. I wasn't ready to do that. He was way too skeptical of all things supernatural. Why risk losing him? Things were good the way they were. "We found this lost cat tonight and this is the address on her collar." I pointed to the end condo. "But, no one is answering the door."

"Well, I'm not sure there's anything I can do here." Will stroked the cat, his clear blue eyes full of unasked questions. "You'll probably just have to wait until they come home."

"But, the cat was traumatized by the sn—"

"Scenario." I jumped in, cutting Mallory off again. "Yeah, some scenario that happened inside has her really freaked out. You should check it out. I think there's something really wrong in there." I snuck a glance at Mallory. She was shaking her head at me. I pleaded with her silently to keep quiet about my snake vision.

Will glanced from me to Mallory and then, sighing, marched up and knocked on the door. No answer. We followed him around back and I showed him the rip in the screen and the knocked over plant.

"All right. Let me talk to the neighbors, see if they've seen the residents around lately."

I knew he was just indulging me, but at this point, I'd take it. We stood behind him as he knocked next door. A large woman answered, her body draped in a flowered nightgown and rollers in her silver hair. Two small Yorkshire terriers circled her feet and yapped at us. She gave Will an appreciative smile as she looked him over and then spotted the black cat in my sister's arms.

"Oh!" She stepped outside, shooing the dogs back in and closing the door on the barking. "Is that Lucky?" she motioned at the black cat, confusion pulling at her gray eyes.

Will glanced at us.

Lucky? I shrugged and nodded.

He turned back to the woman. "Yes, ma'am, seems so." Will held up his badge. "I'm sorry to bother you at this hour, but I'm Detective Blake. We were wondering if you've seen your neighbor lately. These ladies tried to return this lost cat but there's no answer."

"Huh. That's odd." She turned to look at the silent residence. "Well, there's only one woman who lives there, Rose Faraday. I haven't seen her since Sunday. Which is kind of strange." She stared at the cat thoughtfully. "She wouldn't have let Lucky outside the lanai. She must have escaped somehow and Rose would'a been tearing up this town lookin' for her." She folded fleshy arms over her chest. "I'll tell you what I do know, though. I've been complaining to my husband about a foul odor today. It seems to be coming from her side of the wall. She must be doing some kind of weird mumbo jumbo over there."

I noticed Will stiffen. "Okay, thank you, ma'am. We'll check it out."

We had to hustle to keep up with Will as he strode back to his car and radioed dispatch for backup.

"That's bad, right?" I asked. "The foul odor?"

He stepped back out of the car and stared at Rose Faraday's front door. "Can be, yeah." He turned his attention back on us. I saw the concern now fully manifested in the crinkles around his eyes. "Why don't you go on home. I'll give you a call when we know something."

Oh my stars. Now what? I couldn't let Will and the other officers go in there without knowing there may be a poisonous snake on the loose. I couldn't say, "Hey, watch out for the poisonous snake either". I had really gotten myself in a pickle this time.

"All right," I said, buying time. "We'll leave when the other officers get here." I glanced at Mallory. She tilted her head and grinned at me. Obviously enjoying the little predicament my refusal to let Will in on my secret had gotten me into. I fought the urge to stick my tongue out at her. I couldn't let Will see me acting like a five year old. Why does my family bring out the child in me?

It only took two units a few minutes to arrive. I watched them roll up and groaned. I hadn't had time to come up with a plan yet. They parked behind Will's sedan and four officers joined Will in the small square of front yard. As Will filled them in, Mallory leaned over and whispered to me.

"You're not going to let your boyfriend go in there with a poisonous snake possibly on the loose, are you?"

"He's not my boyfriend, Mal and... I'm thinking." *Was he my boyfriend?* My stomach flopped. No, I couldn't call him my boyfriend with the big secret I was hiding from him. We were just dating.

Enjoying each other's company. My guilt receded slightly. I shook those thoughts off. I had to focus on the snake issue.

Will gave me a thumbs up as they headed in. I waved back, panic starting to tickle my insides. I had to think fast. "Give me Lucky." I hefted the cat into my arms, holding her tight so her protesting squirming didn't make me drop her. I crept up the driveway as they worked on opening the door.

Crack! The officers popped the door opened.

"Whoa!" They all took a step back, covering their noses and drawing their guns. Will stepped through the front door behind them. One of them called out, identifying the group as police officers.

This was it. I had to do something. I ran up and sat Lucky in the doorway. Then I screamed as only a southern gal can and scooped her back up into my arms. Her large round eyes stared at my face, ears back. I was pretty sure if cats could talk, this one would ask me if I had lost my mind.

The officers wheeled around, startled. "She tried to run in!' I pointed into the living room. "Snake! I just saw a big snake!" Then I took a few steps backwards, off the porch and out onto the lawn. Thankfully they all followed me.

"Darwin, are you sure? It's pretty dark in there," Will said, his voice full of skepticism.

"Yes! I know a snake when I see one." I was stroking the cat nervously, hoping to heavens if the snake had escaped again, and wasn't still in the house, this wouldn't be another notch on the crazy belt for me in Will's eyes.

"What kind of snake?" One of the officers asked with a touch of panic in his voice.

I closed my eyes and recalled the vision from Lucky. "Dark colored with white patterns on it. Big. Very big." I opened my eyes, hoping that was enough information for them to know it was the dangerous kind.

They had re-holstered their weapons and were staring at Will, waiting for a verdict.

Finally, Will nodded. "All right. Something has definitely gone wrong in there. Let's not take any chances. We'll get a trapper out here to go in first." He walked over and pulled the door closed. I breathed a huge sigh of relief.

As we waited for the trapper, Will and I chatted by his car. "We still on for dinner Saturday night?"

I looked over at Mallory, who was having her own little chat with a young officer. Oh boy, I wasn't sure I could handle Mallory loose in St. Pete. I wasn't sure St. Pete could handle it either. "Sure. I guess I'll have to bring my little sister if she's still here." And just hope that she'd behave herself.

"I don't mind. I enjoy the alone time with you but it'd be nice to get to know someone from your family. Since you never talk about them."

I saw the teasing glint in his eye. There's a reason I don't talk about them. Will has made it clear he doesn't believe in psychics or paranormal stuff of any kind. I'm not ready to possibly lose him over the things about my family I can't control. I made a tactical move and changed the subject. "You don't talk about your family, either."

Before he could answer, a white pick-up truck rambled up and parked in the driveway. A man hopped out wearing cowboy boots, his gray hair pulled back into a ponytail and holding a long, metal stick in his hand. He strode over and held out the other hand to Will.

"Name's Duncan. Someone call about a snake?"

Will shook his hand. "Detective Blake." Then he pointed to Rose's condo. "We're not positive, but don't want to take any chances. Miss Winters here thinks she saw a large, dark snake with a white pattern in the living room. We're not sure if the owner of the condo is home. There's been a report of a foul odor from her residence and no one has seen her for a few days. So..." Will's mouth pinched into a worried line.

"Gotcha." The man said, nodding. "All righty. I'll check it out." The other officers gathered around as we all watched him open the door.

"Pfffweeey!" His reaction easily carried through the night air. He pulled the bandana around his neck up over his nose and then disappeared inside.

Some of the other neighbors had started coming out to see what all the fuss was about. Will questioned them about the last time they saw Rose Faraday. The same answers. Not for a few days.

Suddenly the gathered crowd took a collective breath inward as Duncan stepped back through the door holding up his pole. On the end of it hung a large, fat snake at least seven foot long. Its tail writhed around, rattling angrily.

I glanced at Will. His mouth dropped open. Everyone seemed frozen as Duncan carried the thing over to his truck and pulled a large sack from the back bed. "She's a beaut, eh? Eastern Diamondback," he called. "By the way..." he slipped the bag over the snake and tied it with a yank, then put it in the back of his truck. He walked over to Will and leaned in to him. "I'm sorry to tell ya you got a victim in there. I'm no expert on people, but I know a snake bite when I see one."

"Go." Will nodded to the officers. "Thank you for coming out, Duncan."

"Yep. Good thing you fellows didn't walk in there unaware. This gal is not a happy camper."

Will glanced down at me and smiled gratefully.

I shrugged, though my legs were shaking. *Yeah, good thing.* "So, is this kind of snake common in this area?" I asked Duncan.

"I wouldn't say common but not unheard of. We got a ten footer crossing the street about ten miles north of here. They're losing their natural habitat so man's going to have more and more run-ins with 'em."

Darn. So, finding the snake didn't prove that someone let it in the condo on purpose. Will could feasibly believe it made it in there on its own. "What's going to happen to the snake now?"

"I've got a buddy with a license to house poisonous reptiles. I'll take her on over to him. She'll be part of public education."

After Duncan drove off with the murder weapon, the officers came back out and confirmed Rose Faraday's demise.

"She definitely was bitten by the rattlesnake. No cage, so don't think it was a pet. I'll call in the

ME and crime scene unit," one of the officers said. The mood was low.

"I'll be here for awhile." Will rubbed my arm. "I'll call you later, okay?"

"Yeah, guess we'll head out." I gave him a small smile. Another truck pulled up. A reporter. Yep, time to get out of here.

"Fisch, let's get the crime scene tape up," Will called.

"Good luck." I gave him a quick kiss goodbye and we headed out.

CHAPTER FIVE

The next morning brought Frankie into the boutique with a newspaper in her hand. "Darwin! Looks like you had an exciting night, child. Why didn't you call me?"

Frankie had quickly become one of my dearest friends since moving here. She was a former homeless woman who had won the lottery. She deserved it. She had a heart of gold, despite her eccentricities. Normally I welcomed her enthusiasm, but I was still working on my first cup of tea so I wasn't feeling like the sharpest tool in the shed. Lucky had howled most of the night and the emergency flower essence only succeeded in expanding the times between crying, not stopping it. My brain was still in first gear.

As I stared at her over the counter, Frankie smoothed out the front page of the paper in front of me. There was a photo of Rose Faraday's condo draped in police tape. Inlaid in the corner of the shot was a picture of Rose, obviously done professionally. She looked to be about in her fifties, a bit on the chunky side with dark eyes and dark hair. I skimmed the article, seeing my name mentioned as the person who found her cat and alerted the authorities.

"How did they know my name?" I groaned. When Will called me late last night, he assured me he didn't give them my name. Notoriety was something I tried to avoid in this town. I had enough of that back in Savannah.

Two more of our regular customers rushed through the door. "Darwin, we want the whole scoop."

Frankie chuckled and shot me a sympathetic smile. "Try to think of it as free advertising."

"There really is no scoop, ladies." I shrugged. "My sister and I found Rose's cat last night and tried to return it to her. Her neighbor told Detective Blake that Rose hadn't been seen in a few days and, when she mentioned a suspicious smell, Will called for backup. They went in and found out she had been... deceased."

"Did you say 'your sister'?" Frankie asked.

I nodded and tried not to roll my eyes. "I'll fill you in later."

"Aren't you leaving out one very weird point?" Sarah Applebaum squealed, squeezing her Shih Tzu protectively to her chest. "Death by snake bite in her own house? Just freaky. What are the odds?"

"Gawd, could you imagine?" Patrice Patterson scoffed. "You think you're safe in your own home. Then bam... some crazy thing like a snake attack." Patrice raised exotic birds which, with her beaklike nose and small black eyes, seemed very fitting.

"You're so right." I thought maybe it would be a good idea after all to push the "freakish" thing. Someone needed to investigate this further. If I couldn't make the authorities suspicious, that someone would have to be me. Again. "I didn't think of it that way, Patrice, but it is a freak thing. How do you suppose a snake could get into someone's home anyway? Seems very unlikely."

Another customer came through the door, joining in the conversation. This was going to be a long day. I heard Sylvia's heels clicking on the floor behind me as she came out of the back.

"I say she was cursed." Sylvia threw in when she heard our topic. "Playing around with those psychic things. Is not good idea."

I lifted my head. "She was a psychic?"

"Obviously not a very good one," Sarah chuckled. "Didn't see that coming."

"Sarah!" Patrice said, though she was trying to fight a smirk. "Respect for the dead."

"That was how she made a living, yeah," Frankie offered. "She did tarot card readings at parties. I never met her, but she was recommended to me by my masseuse. Said she was always dead on." Frankie's face drained at her choice of words. "I mean... accurate. Lord have mercy. I'm gonna get a cup of tea. Wake up my brain."

"Well, I think it's strange that it happened around the devil's holiday! And by a "serpent"? Tell me that's not symbolic!" Patrice's brow raised.

"Oh, poo, Halloween is not the devil's holiday, Patrice." Sarah rolled her eyes. "Don't be so superstitious."

"Oh yeah, then why the increase in weird things happening?" She reached over and flipped the paper to an inside section, tapping it with an acrylic nail. "Did you see this at the Travelers Palm Inn last night?"

I glanced down, did a double take and cringed. It was a photo of the energy ball Mallory had created. This instant journalism thing with cell phones was getting really out of hand.

"Someone on one of those ghost tours snapped this last night. A big ball of fire that tried to attack them. How do you explain that?" Patrice gave the growing crowd of women a self-satisfied smile.

"On Halloween, the devil comes and gives you bad luck," one of the newcomers offered.

Attacked them? Bad luck? Oh good heavens. Should I tell them I was there and dispel the whole attack thing? No, I decided. Better to not be attached to another weird story. I kept silent.

By the end of the morning, I was on edge from the stream of questions. The pet boutique had stayed busy with people who wanted the scoop on Rose's death. I wanted to strangle that reporter. At least some of them actually purchased items while digging for information. One of Rose Faraday's neighbors even ordered a birthday cake, one of my newest experiments, for her ten year old Schnauzer. I guess snooping was good for the pet boutique's business after all.

In the afternoon Mallory grew bored hanging out by herself upstairs and decided to help me in the boutique. After her enthusiastic account of our ghost hunting experience to a few customers, I sent her back up to the townhouse to make some Halloween decorations for the boutique windows.

Creativity was her strong point. Thinking before speaking was not.

CHAPTER SIX

By Friday, Sylvia and I were exhausted. We were falling behind on tasks like unpacking shipments and tracking inventory and the place was a wreck. We had decided we would need to hire someone for seasonal help. Mallory was great with the customers and had learned how to ring up their purchases, but I still felt uneasy having her around. To me, she was like a time bomb just waiting to blow up any sense of normalcy in my new life here.

Friday evening, I stood in the kitchen opening a can of tuna while Lucky perched on the kitchen bar, staring up at me with those intense eyes, mewing loudly. She was either complaining that we left her alone today, or I wasn't wielding the can opener fast enough.

Mallory sat on the bar stool, stroking her guitar and humming. She paused at one of Lucky's more insistent yowls. "Hey, we should get her a scratching post or something. I bet she gets bored."

I glanced up sharply. "Lucky can't stay here, Mal." What I meant was Mallory couldn't stay here. Her use of the word "we" had got my shackles up. I loved her but I really needed her to buy a return ticket home.

"Where's she going to go? You know how hard it is to adopt out black cats. Especially traumatized ones."

Mallory had a point. Lucky moved about the townhouse by vaulting from the furniture and counters, or by Mallory carrying her around. She wouldn't actually walk on the floor. Besides still crying off and on through the night, she jumped at every noise, like the refrigerator kicking on. "I was thinking you could take her back home with you. Since the only time she comes near me is when I'm opening her tuna can."

Mallory stopped strumming to throw me one of her signature eye rolls. "Oh yeah, I'm sure Mom would just love for me to bring another cat in the house."

"You know Mom can't say no to you. You can talk her into anything." I felt Mallory's energy heat up. Offended. Changing the subject, I watched Lucky delicately mouth the tuna. Seemed like it was the only time she could really forget about the rotten luck in her life recently. "Hey, I have to make a birthday cake tonight for Mrs. Shoster's shnauzer, Snookie."

"Ha! Say that five times fast." Mallory snorted.

I returned her smile as I pulled out a bag of organic carrots. "Grate these for me while I mix up the rest of the ingredients, would you?"

I preheated the oven and retrieved a large glass mixing bowl from the cabinet. As I pulled eggs from the fridge and peanut butter, rice flour and vegetable oil from the pantry, Mallory shook her head. "Good grief, Darwin, is Mrs. Shoster going to feed this cake to her human friends, too?"

I scooped out a big glob of peanut butter. "If they're brave enough to try it, they certainly could."

Mallory's cell phone rang. She wrapped the washed carrots up in a dishtowel so nosey Lucky wouldn't start nibbling on them and pulled her phone from her pocket.

"Hey, Willow. What's up?"

My heart felt like a giant fist was squeezing it as Mallory walked into the living room to talk to our sister. I dabbed at my eyes with a dishtowel. We had all been so close before I left Savannah and now Mallory was the only one speaking to me. I wasn't so sure her motives were pure, either. *Was she just here to spy on me? To ruin it for me so I had to come crawling back to Savannah?*

I chastised myself and squashed that thought. No matter how mad my family was at me, I knew they wouldn't sabotage my happiness. Not on purpose anyway. I sighed and envied Lucky as she began the process of her after meal bath, her rough pink tongue starting with a paw. If only life were just about eating, bathing and sleeping, how simple it would be.

When Mallory came back to the kitchen, she was quieter.

"Everything okay?" I asked, turning off the mixer.

"Yeah, fine. Just..." she began grating the carrots over a bowl. "Grandma Winters had a small accident. Fractured her wrist in a fall. She was supposed to visit at the end of the month, but that'll be postponed."

"Oh, that's terrible." I cracked an extra egg into the batter. "She knows I left home, I assume?"

"Yep." Mallory used her elbow to nudge Lucky away from the bowl. "She hasn't said anything about it one way or the other though. If you were wondering."

I nodded. If there was one person I didn't want mad at me, it was Grandma Winters. I would have to remember to send her a get well card and one of these days stop being such a scaredy-cat and give her a call.

I hadn't noticed how dark it had gotten in the place until a row of candles on the far end of the bar sparked and ignited one after the other. I raised an eyebrow at my sister.

"Mal, you can't do stuff like that around here." I didn't mention how impressed I was. She'd obviously been practicing since I left.

"It's just us," she sighed, grating the carrots faster. "I don't understand why you're so embarrassed, you know if people could choose to have magick they would in a heartbeat."

"It's not that simple. People judge those who are different. They fear what they don't understand. Don't you ever get tired of being judged and treated like a pariah in Savannah?"

"Nope," Mallory said, handing me the bowl of grated carrots. "I could care less what people think about me or our family. I guess that's the difference between us."

Sighing, I shook the carrots into the mix and stirred. Mallory went back to playing her guitar. Lucky had her back legs stretched out, working on bathing her underbelly with her pink, sandpaper tongue. I poured the mix into a fire hydrant shaped cake pan and popped it into the oven. Mrs. Shoster wanted it delivered at noon tomorrow. She lived three condos down from where Rose Faraday had lived. I thought about that large snake pulled from her condo, wriggling on the end of the trapper's pole. Someone had let it in there on purpose. Who would do such a thing? And why?

CHAPTER SEVEN

By 11:30 a.m. the yogurt-frosted cake was decorated and packed in a box adorned with blue ribbon, ready to be delivered. Since this was my first cake delivery I had failed to work out one little detail. I didn't have a car. Even if I did, I didn't actually know how to drive so it wouldn't do me much good.

I pulled my bike off the balcony, brought it into the kitchen and rigged a picnic basket to the back of it.

"That's how you make deliveries?" Mallory asked from her perch on the sofa. Both she and Lucky, curled up on her stomach, were staring at me like I had grown an extra head. "You're worried about your reputation here? You look like Dorothy from the Wizard of Oz."

"In case you haven't noticed, Mal, this is St. Pete. There are way more odd characters here than a girl delivering a cake on a bike. I'll be fine."

I slid the cake box into the basket. Perfect fit. "I'll be back in an hour. If you want, we can hit a museum or something before meeting Will for dinner tonight."

"Or we could just lay on the beach like two lazy bohemians."

"Yeah, there's that." I shrugged. Not a bad idea. I could use to recharge my batteries. It had been a harrowing, busy week and exhaustion was beginning to feel like the norm.

It was a gorgeous day for a bike ride. High seventies, low humidity, sunshine. I glided down the quiet street, glad this was a happier occasion than the last time I was here. Finding the right address, I leaned my bike against Mrs. Shoster's porch and lifted out the cake box. My knock brought immediate and incessant barking from the other side of the door.

"Oh, hello, Darwin." Mrs. Shoster answered the door in a flowered dress and an oversized plastic beaded necklace. She pushed Snookie back away from the door with a bare foot. "Well, let her in, Snook, she's bringing your cake for crying out loud." I followed her into the kitchen. "Just set it right there on the counter, sugar."

I was surprised to see that, although the condos looked small from the outside, they were open and rather spacious on the inside. This one had been decorated with smoked glass tables, mirrors on the walls and peach leather furniture. Two ladies holding tea cups waved to me from the sofa by the sliding glass doors. I noticed a Chihuahua peering out from one lady's lap and a small, wiry, brown dog panting at the feet of the other. The smell of cinnamon hung heavy in the air.

"Hi, ladies. I'm Darwin Winters from Darwin's Pet Boutique. Y'all here for Snookie's party?" I smiled.

The thin, red head rolled her eyes and laughed. "We're indulging Jeanie because she's our oldest friend. I'm Gretchen by the way." She patted the Chihuahua in her lap. "This is Tiny Tim."

"Nice to meet you both."

"Mary Beth and Brownie." The younger, plumper woman offered.

"Don't worry." Jeanie Shoster waved a finger at her guests. "I have goodies baking for us humans, too." She flicked on the oven light. "Almost done."

Ah, that was the source of the mouthwatering cinnamon smell. I unboxed the cake.

"Oh, that's just lovely. Wonderful job, Darwin," Jeanie squealed. Snookie had jumped up on her legs to sniff it. "Not yet, snookems." She shooed him down. "Patience!"

"You're not going to make us look at his puppy pictures first, are you?" Gretchen asked.

I noticed Jeanie's face drop so I tried to help her out. "You know, pet birthday parties are all the rage right now. Especially among the upper class families who either didn't have children or their children are grown."

"Is that right?" Gretchen shrugged. "Well, Jeanie is always in the know when it comes to all things pet-related."

Jeanie brightened up and winked at me. "I even made little 'doggie bags' full of treats for them to take home." She clapped. "We're just waiting for two more guests."

Mary Beth groaned. "You didn't invite Tula with that little rat that pees on everything did you?"

"Of course Tula's coming. But," she held up a hand, "she's putting Angel in a diaper."

I folded my arms with a grin. "They make doggie diapers?"

"Sure, in fact, Darwin, you should carry those. We've got a lot of friends with aging dogs around here."

"Not a bad idea." I made a mental note to check into that.

"Maybe we should all keep our pets in diapers instead of letting them do their business outside like nature intended." Gretchen had a little bite to her tone.

"Save us money on that damned DNA testing," Mary Beth said.

"Well, maybe that will get voted down now that You-Know-Who is no longer president," Jeanie said. She made the sign of the cross on her chest.

"DNA testing?" I asked.

"Yeah, the HOA committee decided to combat the fact that pet owners weren't picking up after their pets by doing a DNA sample on any pet waste found. If it's yours, they slap you with a $1,000 fine! And if you don't pay it, they put a lean against your condo."

"Or they can confiscate your pet," Mary Beth threw in.

"Take your pet? Is that even legal?" I asked.

"Well, they can do whatever they want and we had to pay two hundred dollars to put our dog's DNA on file. See here." Jeanie picked up Snookie and held out a little green tag on his collar. "This is his DNA Pet World Registry I.D tag."

I thought about something else Jeanie had said. "Were you talking about Rose Faraday? Was she the association president?"

"Yep," Jeanie answered. "It was all her idea to start this ridiculous program. At least she didn't poison poor Monkey like she threatened to."

I frowned. *She threatened to poison a monkey?*

"I know, can you believe it? She actually said she was gonna feed rat poison to his little rat." Jeanie's hand fluttered to her throat. "I thought Jack was gonna knock her block off when she said that, his face got red as a tomato."

Oh! Monkey must be a dog.

"Yeah, that was an entertaining meeting." Mary Beth shook her head. "Of course, she has... *had* a cat so it didn't affect her."

Jeanie snapped her fingers. "Oh, speaking of her cat, you were taking care of Lucky that night, weren't you, Darwin? How's she doing?"

"Yes." I nodded, still thinking about this Jack person. *Was he mad enough to plant the rattler in Rose's condo?*" She's pretty traumatized. She won't walk on the floor and she cries at night. I think she misses Rose. But, she's gotten quite attached to my sister." So, I was guessing there was no love lost between these ladies and Rose. "Will y'all be attending the service for Rose on Sunday?"

"Oh, is it Sunday?" Jeanie asked. She began to fiddle with something on the counter. "I have a hair appointment... usually takes hours."

The other ladies chuckled.

Ding dong. Snookie's barks echoed off the condo walls.

"Snookems, shush." Jeanie scooted the schnauzer out of the way with her foot so she could open the door. "Oh, Jack, Hello." She kissed his freshly shaved and cologned cheek.

"And hello Monkey." She scratched under the chin of the strange little creature. The dog was hairless except for white tufts on his ankles, tail and top of his head. He had a leather spiked collar around his neck and his tongue hung down the side of his jaw.

"Jack, this is Darwin." She walked him in and introduced us. "She owns Darwin's Pet Boutique on Beach Drive and has made this lovely birthday cake for Snookie."

"Howdy, Darwin. Now that is a fine lookin' cake." He shook my hand. "This here's Monkey, he's a Chinese Crested."

"Nice to meet you." I studied him, looking for anything in his eyes that might suggest he was homicidal. "And you, too, Monkey. I'm sure y'all will enjoy the goodies Jeanie has for you." Jack carried Monkey into the living room and sat him on the floor where he proceeded to sniff around the carpet and then stick his nose up the other dogs' backsides.

"How are we today, ladies?" Jack used the more socially acceptable form of greeting for humans... a handshake.

I noticed a distinct shift of atmosphere in the room. The women became more bubbly and flushed. Was Jack the resident "good catch"? He did still have a full head of silver hair and a confident air about him. The doorbell rang again, bringing

Snookie scrambling on the tile to bark at the intruder. The last guest, Tula, entered holding a nearly hairless, white dog wearing a sweater and a diaper. The dog, not Tula.

I guessed it was time to make my exit and let these nice folks get their party on. I pulled some coupons for free nail trims out of my bag and laid them on the counter. "Here, Jeanie, you can add these to your guests' goodie bags."

"Oh, so thoughtful. Thank you."

I said my goodbyes and left.

On the bike ride back to Beach Drive, I thought about the fact that Rose was the president of the home owners association and how mad all the dog owners were about the implemented doggie DNA program. Seemed like Rose Faraday was enemy number one in her neighborhood, especially if she was threatening to poison people's dogs. *Could that be enough motive for murder?* Depends on exactly how angry people were, I supposed. If someone thought their dog was going to be confiscated, that could do it. Or if they feared for their pet's life. One thing I've learned already from my short time in the pet business. You do not mess with people's animals.

CHAPTER EIGHT

Mallory and I had spent a relaxing day at the beach, soaking ourselves in the sun and water, so by the time six o'clock rolled around, we were experiencing that familiar bond again, laughing and feeling comfortable with each other. Since the tension had eased from our relationship, I was dying to ask her if she had forgiven me for leaving yet, but decided that was a subject best left for another day. When she was ready to bring it up.

We arrived at the Moon Under Water restaurant before Will and waited until a table opened up beneath the burgundy umbrellas.

"This looks like a scene from a Hollywood movie," Mallory commented, surveying the area as we sat down.

"Yeah." I smiled, joining her in assessing our view. "Amazing, isn't it?"

A horse and carriage had parked on the street beside us, a musician played on the porch of the restaurant next door and the Straub Park trees sparkled against the background of Bay waters. A slight breeze rustled the surrounding tropical foliage. I sighed. Paradise. I ordered a merlot and water. Mallory reluctantly ordered an iced tea since she was only eighteen.

"So, what's the deal with you and Mr. Hot-Stuff Detective anyway? It's pretty obvious you two are crazy about each other. Why isn't he your boyfriend?"

"It's complicated." I watched an elderly couple shuffle by, hand in hand, wearing matching Dali museum t-shirts. *Could that be me and Will some day?* I flushed at the thought.

Mallory stared at me expectantly.

"Okay, because I can't let myself get that close to him until..." My eyes welled up. *Heavens, was I more upset about this than I would admit to myself?* "Until I can tell him the truth and not hide secrets from him."

"So don't hide secrets from him." She leaned on her elbows and tilted her head. "You have something in your eye?"

I picked up a napkin and pressed it into the corners of my eyes, ignoring her. "It's not that simple. He's so closed minded, Mal. I've had dreams about telling him. Nightmares, really. He leaves me, disgusted. So, I just can't bring myself to do it, knowing it will be over between us."

"Oh, so you can read people's minds now?" She frowned at me and sighed. "Besides, Grandma Winters says if someone can't love you, warts and all, they don't deserve you."

My turn to sigh. "I know, but I'm hiding some pretty big warts." I really wouldn't blame him for leaving me. That was the problem. I didn't believe I deserved him, not if I couldn't be honest with him.

Mallory sat back in her chair with a frustrated thump. "This place does sort of have its own kind of magic," she said, her voice softening. "I guess I can see why you like it here." Then her mouth curved into a smile. "And why you like him." She nodded behind me.

I turned and caught sight of Will approaching through the crowd. I didn't know if I'd ever stop getting that little flutter in my stomach every time I saw him. His six-four frame looked especially yummy tonight clad in a pair of dark jeans and white linen shirt. I stood to greet him. When he kissed my cheek, I closed my eyes and breathed in his signature scent of fresh rain and coconut. "Hi."

"Hello, gorgeous." He took the seat to my left, letting his hand linger on my back. "Evening." He smiled at Mallory. "So, how are you enjoying St. Pete so far?"

Mallory twisted a tendril of red hair around her finger. "Well, besides my sister making me slave away in her pet boutique, it's been fun."

"Nice, Mal." I rolled my eyes. The waitress brought our drinks and Will ordered a Guinness. "Don't let her fool you. We spent the day lounging on the beach. After I delivered my first pet birthday cake, that is."

"Ah, a day at the beach? That's why you two look so radiant. Well, congratulations on the cake," Will said, smiling at me. "Though, I can't imagine having a birthday cake for a pet. Do people seriously do that?"

Radiant? Yeah. We don't get sunburned or waterlogged; we get powered up like batteries. "It's not so strange. Pets give so much love and companionship to their owners; they just want to give something back. Besides, I think around here it's just another reason to throw a party. Oh, before I forget, Sylvia said Landon's having a Halloween party next Saturday night. Everyone's going to dress up. Can you make it?"

Will's mouth twisted to the side. "A few weeks early, isn't it?"

"Yeah, well, Sylvia says he knows there's going to be other events and parties on the actual Halloween weekend, so he wanted to do it early."

"Well, you'll have to brave this one without me, I'm afraid. Work calls." He slid his hand on top of mine and squeezed apologetically. "Sorry."

I felt a stab of disappointment but I forced it away and concentrated on enjoying the time I did have with Will. With his job, I had to be flexible.

"Who's Landon?" Mallory asked trying to sneak a sip of my wine.

I shooed her hand away. "Landon Stark. He's a magician and Sylvia's boyfriend," I said.

"Like, a *real* magician?" Mallory smirked at me. I kicked her under the table. "What?" she frowned. "Just asking."

Yeah, I knew what she was asking. Our mother had been seventeen when she snuck out to a magic show with her friends. Turned out, that night changed the course of her life. The superstar "magician" was our father, Ash Winters, and his magick was real. He picked her out of the crowd for a disappearing trick and immediately fell for her. They saw each other secretly for three months until she got pregnant with me. Her very strict, religious parents weren't having any of it and kicked her out, so our father moved her to his family mansion in Savannah, where he would visit her every few years, leaving her with two more girls four years apart. Mom seemed to understand this arrangement, though she would never elaborate on it. She would just sigh and start to say something about "the law of three" and then stop herself. The one time I had tried to really push her for information, her eyes grew so sad, I decided not to ask again.

The waitress brought Will's drink and took our orders.

I straightened up, pushing the past aside. "So, I heard Rose Faraday's funeral is tomorrow?" I glanced at Will.

"Is it?" he asked. Then he looked at me curiously. "You didn't know her. Are you planning on attending?"

"Well." I shrugged. "I am taking care of her cat. I was thinking maybe I could find one of her relatives at the service who would like to adopt Lucky."

Will took a sip of his Guinness. I had an urge to lick the foam off his upper lip but he beat me to it. "Oh. I forgot about her cat. Good plan."

I stifled a smile and blinked my eyes innocently at him. "Or you could take her. You did say you would get a new cat." His wife had left him six years ago and took their cat.

His mouth twisted in a grin as he leaned over and kissed me lightly on the lips. "I said I *could* get a new cat. There's a difference."

"Oh," I whispered, our lips still in close proximity. "But she's a very nice cat."

"I don't have time for a cat." He kissed me again.

I could have spent all evening talking about the cat but Mallory cleared her throat. We sat back and looked at her.

Mallory was making a face at me.

"What's wrong, Mal?"

"There's no sugar in this iced tea."

I almost laughed because she looked so stunned. Instead, I pushed a few sugar packets her way. "You have to ask for sweet tea in Florida." I turned back to Will, ignoring her grumbling. "Did you know Rose was the president of the HOA at her condos?" I asked, trying to seem uninterested.

"Yes, one of her neighbors mentioned that." Will stared at my mouth, hungrily. I ignored that, too.

"And Jeanie Shoster said that everyone was pretty upset with her for the Doggie DNA registry program she had forced on them."

"Really?" Will's eyes sparkled like they did when he knew I was about to amuse him with something, which apparently I did quite often. "Doggie DNA?"

"Yep. Seems they make everyone register their dog's DNA and if they don't clean up after their pet, they can find out who the culprit is and fine them."

"So someone does a DNA test on the dog poop?" Will shook his head. "Seriously? It's hard enough for us to get timely DNA tests from crime scenes."

"Regardless, I can see why they wouldn't think too kindly of Rose. The fine is $1,000 and if they don't pay it, they can put a lean on their condo or even confiscate their dog! How crazy is that?"

"Well, I agree that's just..." Will searched for the right word but could only grin. "Silly."

I had to get him to take this more seriously. It was the only motive I had so far for someone letting that rattlesnake into Rose's condo.

"I'm sure she had more than a few enemies over this. You can't mess with people's pets, Will. They're like their children."

"Oh, I don't know. Her neighbors had nothing but nice things to say about her."

"Of course they did. It's bad juju to talk ill of the newly departed."

The waitress appeared with our dishes: vegetable curry for me, beef tips for Will and jerk chicken sandwich for Mallory.

Mallory munched on a fry. "Freaky that a rattlesnake could get into a condo all by itself, though, huh, Will?"

I kicked Mallory under the table again. *Did this child not understand subtlety?*

She glanced at me sharply and the candle in the middle of our table flared up.

"Whoa!" Will sat back as the flame—and my sister—settled back down.

"Bit windy tonight." I forced a smile. Mallory wouldn't look at me.

Will glanced at the plants, which were only slightly swaying. "Well, this is Florida. Alligators in pools, snakes in garages... lots of wildlife to contend with."

I sighed and resigned myself to the fact I was going to need more information to make him suspicious enough to investigate Rose's death as murder.

CHAPTER NINE

Sunday morning, our cab pulled up to the Memorial Chapel. Mallory coaxed Lucky gently back into the cat carrier and blew a stray strand of hair from her eye. Lucky meowed in protest. She was much happier on Mallory's lap.

"This is for your own safety," Mallory whispered into the carrier. Then to me, "You owe me for this one, Sis."

"I don't know why you're making such a big deal out of coming with me." I shot her a look as I dug some cash out of my straw bag and handed it to the driver. "Thank you."

She grumbled something about hating funerals as she slid out of the cab without the carrier. I grabbed Lucky, wrestled the carrier out of the seat and met her at the front doors. "There's not even a dead body. She's already been cremated. It's just a ceremony."

A guy in a gray silk suit opened the door for us and smiled politely. "Welcome."

"Hi, we're here for the Rose Faraday memorial," I said, squashing the irritation I had with Mallory.

"Certainly, just follow the hallway out..." he stopped and bent over to stare into the cage.

"Is that a cat?"

"Yes," I said, shifting Lucky to the other hand.

"Well." He straightened up slowly, glancing behind him. "It's very unorthodox to bring a cat to a funeral service. I don't think I can allow it."

I could tell he wasn't sure what to do with me. By his tight frown, I knew I was going to have to do some persuading. "Oh, it's okay." I put on my brightest smile. "This is... I mean, *was*... Rose Faraday's cat, Lady Luck. Rose contacted me and asked me to please bring her today to give the poor thing closure. She's been very upset. The cat, not Rose, obviously. Not eating, crying all the time. She won't even walk on the floor." I lowered the carrier, hoping he wouldn't see Lucky's robust figure.

"Miss Faraday... contacted you?" His face contorted in confusion. "I don't understand."

"Mmhm. Came to me in a dream last night. You know she was a psychic, right?" I moved in closer to him so I could whisper. "Psychics can do that when they pass, you know. Get a message to someone."

"I see." He glanced at Mallory and I had to give her credit. She nodded solemnly, though I could tell from her pinked cheeks she was about to bust.

"Well, I suppose since the ceremony is outdoors." He was still staring at me suspiciously. "Just make sure the cat stays in the cage. We don't want any accidents in the Cremation Garden."

"Of course." I nodded. "Thank you for your understanding. And the Cremation Garden would be?"

"Follow the hallway through the double doors then follow the stone path, stay to the right at the fork."

"Thank you." We hurried down the hall, through the assault of elevator music and an overactive Glade plug in.

Mallory snorted as we hit the stone path. "Ha, I can't believe you lied to the man like that, Sis. I'm so proud of you."

I switched Lucky's carrier to the other arm. For a ball of fur, she was heavy. "Yeah, well. It was for a good cause." I should have taken off my sweater. The October sun had already melted the slight chill from the morning air.

"Cause you're trying to pawn Lucky off on some poor unsuspecting relative?"

I smiled back at her. "Exactly."

The path led us around the edge of a more traditional cemetery with its gray stones and statues, toward a lake where folding chairs sat under a temporary polyester canopy, waiting for occupants. We detoured into the grass and slid into the back row of the chairs. A few people sat quietly in the front row, a few were peppered throughout the other seats and a tall man in a black suit stood beside a table with a china urn resting on top of it. He was engaged in conversation with another man in a black cowboy hat.

"Not many people here," Mallory whispered. "That lady up front with the black feather in her hair looks like a cat person."

"Yeah." I frowned. It was kind of sad Rose didn't have more friends. That would make it more difficult to find out who might have wanted to cause her harm, too. "Maybe we should sit closer so we can chat with her. Come on."

I slid out of the seat and moved down the center aisle, between the chairs. I was almost at the row behind the feather lady when the tall man beside the table suddenly turned his head and met my eyes. A chill ran down my spine and I stopped in my tracks. Mallory ran into my back.

"Hey! What'd you stop for?" she complained. Then I felt her peer over my shoulder. "Oh."

The man's eyes were large black almonds and I could feel his stare like a physical force holding me. He touched the cowboy's arm and then moved toward us without breaking eye contact. Within a few smooth steps, he stood in front of me holding out his hand. I took it and held his gaze, trying to act nonchalant even though my insides were humming. I could feel Mallory pressing up against my back.

His hand was dry and warm. No, more than warm, exuding heat. The crisp black suit jacket seemed to barely contain his chest and arms as they bulged against it. The muscles in his thick neck and chiseled jaw were taut. An aura of power rolled off of him in waves, making me a bit dizzy with fear. It was like coming face to face with an unpredictable, wild animal.

"Zach Faraday." His full lips curved into a smile, though it didn't reach those dark eyes. "And you are?"

"Nobody." I cleared my throat, pulling my hand from his. He reluctantly let go. "I mean, nobody important. Um, Darwin Winters." *Good heavens, get your thoughts together Darwin.* "This is my sister, Mallory." It didn't go unnoticed by me that my usually chatty, nosey sister was staying silent.

He nodded at Mallory. "How did you know my mother?"

My mouth opened and closed a few times. "Oh... Rose is... was your mother?"

"Yes."

"Well, we didn't know her personally. We found her cat, Lady Luck." I held up the carrier and peeked in. Lucky was staring at Zach with wide eyes and ears flattened down on her head. A hiss escaped her. I quickly lowered the carrier again. "We thought maybe Rose had a relative that would like to adopt her. I'm sure your mother would have preferred Lucky to be with someone she knew."

Zach smiled slightly. "Well, unfortunately, I'm her only surviving relative and," he glanced down at the carrier, "I'm allergic to cats. But, a few of the ladies she played bridge with are here. You could talk to them about adopting Lucky."

Why did Lucky dislike Rose's son so much? "Oh, okay. We'll do that after the service, thanks." I wanted to move, wanted to be released from his presence but I felt like I needed permission. "I'm very sorry for your loss," I added.

"Thank you." He nodded, turned as if to go, then stopped and turned back to me. Leaning in close to my ear, he chuckled deeply. "I know what you are." With that, he made his way back to the podium and placed his hands on the urn, his head bowed.

I forced my jelly legs to carry me into a chair and plopped down with Lucky's carrier on my lap. Mallory slid next to me and grabbed my arm.

"What in hell's bells was that? What did he say to you?"

I could tell from her breathlessness that she was as shaken as I was. "He said I know what you are." I watched Mallory's freckles pop out as her face paled. She stared at me, emotions churning in her green eyes—confusion, fear, then anger.

"Impossible. And anyway, so what if he does?" She turned her gaze on him as he began to speak. I felt her shiver. "There's something about him, though. I sensed fire. But, he's not one of us." She shook her head. "Impossible."

Apparently, not all that impossible. The question was, what was he?

"Hi, I want to thank you all for coming here today to celebrate my mother's life and to say goodbye to an amazing woman." He continued his speech and never once glanced our way again.

As I began to recover from our encounter, questions formed.

What exactly did he think I was? A psychic like his mother? Did he inherit his mother's psychic ability, if she truly had any? But most importantly, why was I so sure that he was powerful... and dangerous? If I could have, I would have hightailed it out of there right then. But, I was here to find Lucky a home. We'd just have to stay until we could talk to Rose's bridge friends.

It seemed everyone present wanted their turn at the podium. I was suddenly glad she didn't have more friends. The last speaker, feather lady—Vera Groves—was apparently Rose's bridge partner and a big fan of being in the spotlight. Small as it was.

When she was finally finished with her dramatic, teary speech, Zach thanked her and held his hands out to us all.

"My mother chose a niche bench as her final corporal resting place. If you follow me, I'll show you where it is located so you can visit with her at your convenience." He led the small knot of people toward the lake and under a heavy shade tree. A pair of ducks waddled away from us and slid smoothly into the water. Our small crowd gathered around as Zach slid the urn in a hollowed out part of the pedestal. "Rest in peace, Mother."

After a few moments of silence, Mallory nudged me. Vera Groves and two other women had strayed away from the group. We hurried to catch up with them. The carrier slowed me down a bit, but they still weren't hard to catch.

"Ms. Groves?" I called, waving my arm.

They all turned to me, faces drawn. "Yes?" Vera Groves asked, eyeing me suspiciously.

"Hi, my name's Darwin. I own Darwin's Pet Boutique on Beach Drive, and my sister and I found Rose's cat, Lucky." I lifted the carrier and peeked in. Good, Lucky had her ears up and her eyes halfway closed. Uninterested. Better than freaked out. "To make a long story short, we were hoping that someone close to Rose would adopt Lucky. We think that Rose would have preferred this, rather than Lucky living with strangers."

The women glanced at each other and then at Vera. She was smiling kindly, wiping at her nose with a Kleenex. "Oh, that's a good idea. She loved that cat. Hello, Lucky." She bent over and smiled at the cat. "I'm afraid I can't take her though. I have two dogs that would think I brought them home a new chew toy." She glanced at the other ladies. "Jilly? What about you?"

The frail blonde smiled. "No, sorry. My husband forbade me any more pets after Buddy passed. He wants to travel without any strings."

My heart sank. This wasn't looking good. We all stared at the last woman.

"Oh." She shook her head. "Can't have pets in my condo."

"Okay, I understand. Sorry for your loss, ladies."

I sighed as we watched them walk away. "No luck for Lucky."

"Can we go now?" Mallory stood behind me, looking uncomfortable. I turned to see Zach standing alone, his hands shoved in his pockets, staring back at us.

"Yep," I said, backing away. "Let's go."

CHAPTER TEN

I awoke Monday morning with Lucky sleeping on my head like a Russian hat and a slight nagging in my gut from my encounter with Zach Faraday. What a strange man. Shaking it off, I pulled my head out from under Lucky's curled up body and watched her slide down the pillow without waking up. I checked my phone and shut off the alarm. Sure, 5:23 a.m. is a reasonable time to be awake.

"What happened to sleeping with Mallory?" I grumbled at the cat. Then, I felt bad and stroked her ear. I should be grateful she was no longer shunning me. And she would have actually had to climb the stairs herself. That was a good sign.

After a torturously cold shower to speed up the wake-up process, I towel-dried my hair, threw on a silk robe and padded down the stairs, where I found Mallory sitting in the still-dark living room, practicing with a row of candles.

"Hey, what are you doing up so early?" My voice disturbed the silence and startled Mallory. She jumped.

The candles all roared to life at once. "Couldn't sleep."

Now I knew why Lucky ended up in my bed. "Any particular reason?"

"Mm." She shrugged, her eyes never leaving the dancing flames. The middle one stretched up higher and higher, licking the air as if searching for something to consume. "Had a bad dream."

I walked over to stand in front of her. She wouldn't meet my eyes. With her hair all piled on top her head, and wearing pink pajamas with butterflies, she looked much younger than her eighteen years. I felt deeply protective of her and had an urge to wrap my arms around her like I used to when she was little and would sneak into my room after a nightmare. "Want to talk about it?"

"No. Not really."

Lucky had made her way downstairs in stealth mode and used the chairs, bar and then end table to reach the back of the sofa. *Okay, maybe not so much progress.* Could cats get post traumatic stress syndrome? The flower essence wasn't helping her recover from her encounter with the rattlesnake. I'm sure she missed Rose, too. Maybe it was time to try something a bit more powerful. I thought about the chalice Mallory had brought to me. Did I really want to open that can of worms here?

I watched Lucky curl up on the sofa between Mallory and a throw pillow.

Feeling helpless, I decided to back off. "Okay. I'm going to make some tea. Want some?"

"Sure."

I paused and watched her for a moment as she grew each flame in turn, connecting the energy within her that was in tune with the sympathetic resonance of the fire. She made it seem effortless and a part of me yearned to stretch my own wings and practice.

"Hey, Mal?"

A tired sigh escaped her. "Yeah?"

I shifted my feet. "Have you ever dreamed about Father?"

She finally glanced up at me. Her eyes were puffy. They held a touch of surprise. We never talked about our father. She nodded. "Once, on my thirteenth birthday and then..." she looked away and the middle candle flame rose as the others went out. "Then again on the night you left us." She glanced back up at me. "You?"

I hugged my arms around my body and nodded. "Recently, when I was—" I stopped. Telling her I had been in the hospital after being mowed down by a car on purpose would not make her feel better about me leaving Savannah. "When I was really sick. Only, it didn't really seem like a dream. It seemed more like a visit." I smiled. "Except for the weird lady and wolf next to him and the fact that he was under water."

"Really?" Mallory slid back into the sofa and turned her body toward me. "That's how it felt to me, too. In fact, we had this whole conversation and yes, he was under water." She shrugged. "No wolf, though. Or weird lady."

This shocked me. "What did you talk about?"

"Well, this last dream... or visit, whatever it was, I was so upset that you left and he kept telling me everything changes and I had to understand that. He also told me that I had to be strong because you would need me soon and I would know when the right time was to come to you."

I stared at my little sister, trying to piece together this new information. *Our father told her in a dream I would need her?* "So, that's why you came here?"

"Yes," she confessed. "I'm sorry I didn't tell you before." Her eyes were pleading with me not to be angry. "I told Mom about the dream when I felt it was time for me to come here. That's why she let me. That's also why I don't know when I'm going back. I can't go back until whatever you need me for happens."

A chill moved through my body. *Was I in real danger?*

"Mom took the dream seriously, then?"

"Yes."

"Interesting." *Did our father know I was going to be in danger somehow? Does that mean he is watching us from... wherever he is? Or, it could have been just a dream.* But deep inside I knew it was more than that. I didn't know what to say. I needed to do something normal. "I'll get that tea now," I whispered.

I leaned against the stove for support and waited for the kettle to whistle. So many emotions were moving in and out. I tried to just let them flow, feel them and then release them, but the frustration was not cooperating. I moved here to be normal. To have normal friends, a normal quiet life. But, here was my old life and my crazy, absentee father sticking his nose into my new world. No, I wouldn't let that happen. I had to think.

If it was true that I was in danger then it probably came from me trying to solve Rose's murder. I would just have to do that quickly and then Mallory wouldn't worry about me and she could go home.

When I finally returned to the living room with a new resolve and two steaming tea cups, Mallory had her arms crossed, staring at me. Lucky had moved to the back of the sofa and was pulling at Mallory's hair tie. Mallory seemed too focused on being annoyed with me to notice.

"You know, maybe the reason I was sent here to help you is because you won't help yourself. Don't think I haven't noticed that you're not practicing at all. Are you completely shunning everything that Grandma Winters taught you? Everything that our family is about? Father may not be around but he did give us these gifts. The magick is part of our heritage."

According to Mom and Grandma Winters. I still wasn't completely clear on the whole nature of what our father was and what we were. It all seemed like a bad fairytale.

"Mallory, that's not fair. We're human, too. Why can't I just embrace that part of our family?" I put down the cups and fell on the sofa next to her, the frustration reaching new heights. "Will you just try to understand my point of view, please? We were never given a choice growing up if we wanted to be normal or not. But now, I feel like I do have a choice. I have a fresh start. I can be normal here in

St. Pete and that's all I want. Plenty of people live without magick and do just fine. They have friends, hobbies, completely full lives without feeling the need to manipulate nature to get what they want." I saw Mallory's eyes widen and then narrow, but it was too late. I couldn't stop myself. "How do you even know we're supposed to have these gifts? How do we know that those people calling us witches weren't right? Maybe father isn't... maybe these gifts aren't from a good place. Maybe they are—"

"From the devil?" Mallory almost choked on the words, the same ones that people had spit at us growing up, tears springing to her eyes. I immediately wished I hadn't said anything. Too late. "Oh, that's rich, Darwin. Wow." She yanked at her hair tie and her hair tumbled around her shoulders like soft flames. Lucky mewed. Mallory threw the hair tie onto the adjacent love seat and Lucky leaped over the end table to retrieve it.

"No, I didn't say that." I took a shuddering breath. I felt her sense of betrayal blowing through me as waves of heat. Tears were blurring my own vision. I didn't really know what I was saying. I hadn't allowed myself to face my doubts before, to really examine the reason I wanted to leave that side of our family legacy behind. But, I couldn't do it right now either, not under the assault of Mallory's emotional storm. It was too painful. Outside the French doors, the sky was growing lighter. "We'll talk about this later. I have to get ready to open the boutique." I stood on shaky legs and went upstairs, feeling drained and sad.

CHAPTER ELEVEN

The week was a whirlwind. My relationship with Mallory strained against the walls we both had erected and the conversation we were both avoiding. Luckily the pet boutique was slammed. We didn't even have time to go through the applications our 'part-time help wanted' ad had brought in. I told Sylvia I'd take a look at them this weekend but today was Saturday and it was all about getting ready for Landon Stark's Halloween bash.

* * *

We met Sylvia at Gone Retro, a cute little vintage clothing boutique she frequented, to scare up some costumes. Shopping with Sylvia was an educational experience. The woman knew how to find a deal and then make it a bargain. We had only been perusing the costume racks for about fifteen minutes when Sylvia squealed and held up a retro, satin cat-woman costume. Well, costume was an overstatement. It was more like half a costume—a black body suit, faux fur bracelets and matching ears on a headband.

"Darwin, this is puuuurfect for you!" Her dark eyes sparkled mischievously.

After grinning at her and shaking my head, I was talked in to trying it on. To my delight it fit like a glove, the satin material didn't make me itchy and the fur trim around the bust added some volume to my "stick figure," as Sylvia referred to it. I decided adding black tights would be a necessity. But, other than that, I was done.

"Ah, Mallory!" she squealed again a few minutes later. "This! With your gorgeous red hair, this is you, my *amiga*!" She clutched a black mass of lace and tulle to her bosom. "And look. There is a hat!"

Mallory and I exchanged a glance and then we busted out laughing. I felt the tension between us dissolve and my chest loosen.

Mallory's face was flushed, her smile genuine. "It's perfect, Sylvia." She weaved through the rack to accept the find. "I would be honored to be the evening's witch." She smiled back at me. "And Darwin will be my familiar."

I laughed and raised an eyebrow playfully at her.

"You ladies finding everything all right?" The tall, blonde saleswoman approached us after finishing up with another customer.

"I think Sylvia still needs a costume." I pointed to Sylvia, who had her arms buried up to her shoulders in a rack, digging out costumes and then shoving them back in. I wished I had her talent and passion for clothing. She seemed to be having a blast.

"Oh, I think we have the perfect costume for you," the saleswoman said, eyeing Sylvia's figure. She moved behind the counter and pulled out a plastic bag. "This just came back from the seamstress. It was one of my favorite finds."

"Ooooo!" Sylvia gasped as the saleswoman slipped a 60's showgirl green eyelash lamé dress from the bag. "*Espetacula!*"

"Why don't you try it on?" She winked and pointed to the dressing room.

When Sylvia emerged from the dressing room, we all shared her smile. "Wow!" It hugged her curves perfectly; the black sequined fringe lined the bra area and her bottom, swishing just below her hips.

"Add some black silk gloves and a mask." The saleslady nodded. "You'll be stunning."

We went to lunch together at Bella Brava, all giddy from our great finds, and stuffed ourselves silly with their delicious Toscana woodstone oven flatbreads.

"Landon's party is going to be magical," Sylvia gushed around a mouthful of tiramisu.

She had no idea how right she was.

CHAPTER TWELVE

We arrived together, Landon spotting us immediately as we entered the dining room where he usually performed his magic shows. He made his way through the already crowded place, a vampire cape floating behind him.

"Look at you girls!" he beamed, taking one of Sylvia's hands and making her do a little circle spin for him. "You are a vision, my dear." He kissed her lips lightly, being mindful of the fake blood on his own mouth. Her eyes sparkled behind the black sequined mask as he growled, "Be careful, I bite." He snuggled her neck beneath her silky black hair.

"Later." She swatted him playfully. "I want you to meet Darwin's sister, Mallory."

"Ah! Nice to meet you, Mallory." He bowed and then shook her hand. "Landon Stark."

"You're a magician, right?" Mallory asked.

"Guilty as charged." He looked her over, from hat to pointy black boots. "And you are a witch?"

She laughed. "Guilty as charged."

"Well." He motioned for us to follow him. "Let's get you gals a drink."

We weaved our way through the crowd to the bar. He had really outdone himself with the

Halloween theme. The floor was covered in a layer of thick fog from dry ice; carved pumpkins, glowing with candles, served as table centerpieces; giant black spiders hung from the ceiling and eerie music played beneath the conversations around the dim room.

"Darwin!" Frankie rushed towards me, dressed as a short, plump Cruella Deville. She hugged me with one arm, the other arm raised high to protect her drink. "Oh, look at you, you little minx!"

"And look at you," I laughed. "You found the creepiest of creepy costumes."

"And Sylvia." She one-arm hugged her, too. "Whoa, Landon, you better not let her out of your sight tonight. Sexy." She moved her attention to Mallory and grinned. "Hi, I'm Frankie."

Mallory shook her hand. I saw her eyes widen at the large diamond and ruby rings adorning Frankie's hand. "Mallory. Darwin's sister."

"Oh, Darwin's sister." She stepped in and squeezed Mallory in a hug. "Glad to finally meet you."

"You, too," Mallory said, readjusting her hat with a slight grin directed at me.

I shrugged and smiled at her. Frankie's enthusiasm knew no bounds. They should get along fine.

"Here you go, my dears," Landon said, handing Sylvia and me some sort of black cocktail, rimmed in red sugar. "A Devil's Blood cocktail for the lovely ladies." He glanced at Mallory. "Would you like a Sprite?"

I put an arm around her as she opened her mouth to protest. "Yes, she would."

"What is in this?" Sylvia sniffed it suspiciously.

"Blavod Black vodka, cranberry juice... and of course," his voice downshifted into his best vampire impersonation, "blood."

Sylvia pulled the cherry off the clear plastic skull stick and grinned at him. "Of course."

"After that you must try one of these." Frankie lifted her flute. It was white on the bottom and orange on top. "Candy corn." She waved at the bartender. "I have no idea what's in it, but it's delicious. Oh," she whirled around, "wait, I want you to meet my date." She waved at a silver-haired man dressed as Zorro. He excused himself from a conversation he was having with a mummy and came over.

"Jack, I want you to meet my friends. This is Sylvia." He shook her hand, as they exchanged pleasantries. "And—"

"Darwin, right?" He turned to me, smiling. "A man could never forget a name or face like yours. Nice to see you again."

"You, too," I said, suddenly remembering where I had seen him before. Jeannie Shoster's dog birthday party. *Frankie's date, huh?* That pushed him higher on the suspect list. Frankie didn't have the best track record in picking nice guys. "How's Monkey?"

"Neurotic, but that's what I love about him," he said with a chuckle.

I nodded and forced a smile. *Love him enough to kill Rose for threatening to poison him?*

Landon reached for Sylvia's hand. "Folks, I'm going to steal my lovely date away for a moment." Landon smiled down at Sylvia. "Come on, I want to introduce you to someone."

"You girls have fun," she whispered, grinning as she passed me and holding up her glass.

"Happy haunting." I smiled back at her, holding up my own glass. Then, turning to Frankie, I motioned toward the stage where there seemed to be some breathing room. "Let's get out of the crowd." Jack and Mallory followed us to a less dense area of the room.

As we settled in, a young man dressed as Frankenstein approached us with a tray of hors d'oeuvre. He held up the tray with a moan. I gave him an approving once over. Way to stay in character.

"Ha, deviled eggs. Seems like the devil's in everything tonight." Frankie laughed, plucking one up with her free hand and winking at Jack. "Mmm." She took a bite and nodded at us. "Wow, try one, there's caviar in the filling." She held one up to Jack's mouth.

We all took one to try. "So, Jack," I said, swallowing the lump and deciding I didn't really like caviar. "Monkey doesn't happen to like cats, does he?"

He chewed and gave Frankie a thumbs up. "I'm not sure," he said, pushing the Zorro mask up onto the top of his head. "He's never been around one. Why do you ask?"

"Well, I'm trying to find a home for Rose Faraday's cat, Lady Luck."

"Oh, no, sorry, I couldn't. No offense to the poor cat, but I wouldn't bring anything that woman owned into my home."

I was surprised at the level of anger still evident in his tone. After all, the woman was dead. Maybe it was time to let it go.

"Tragic how she died." Frankie shook head. "I still can't believe it."

"Beyond believable," Mallory piped in.

Jack shrugged. "Seems like karma to me."

Karma? How is getting bit by a rattlesnake in your own living room karma? No one deserves that. "So, I heard Rose had threatened to poison Monkey?" I watched his expression. I wasn't disappointed. His eyes flashed with rage. Definitely not ready to let it go.

"Yeah." His face darkened. "I don't know what that woman had against dogs. She went out of her way to make us dog owners' lives miserable there."

The crowd seemed to be getting louder. I had to yell above the din of conversation and music around us. "So she wasn't well liked?"

"I can't speak for the rest of the world, but in our little corner, nope."

I leaned in closer to Jack so my voice wouldn't get drowned out. "Besides the whole dog thing, do you think people resented her occupation? Her being a psychic?" In the back of my mind, I knew I wasn't just asking about Rose here.

"Oh, no, that just made her strange, not a bitch." He glanced at Mallory sheepishly. "Excuse my language, Miss." Then turned back to me. "You know, it was the whole dog DNA mess. That was all her idea as president, and it just rubbed everyone the wrong way."

"Dog DNA?" Frankie made a face. "What's this world coming to? But, now that you've been elected president of the HOA, you can change whatever you need to, right?"

That got my attention. *Jack was the new president?* Bing. Moving on up the suspect list. Short as it was so far.

"Oh, yeah. You bet your sweet buns we're working on changing that!" Jack answered.

I felt a bit of relief that they didn't dislike her just for being a psychic. Time for the big question to see how he reacted. "So, Jack, do you think anyone disliked her enough to kill her?"

He paused midway of taking a drink and stared at me. Then one side of his mouth twitched. "You mean if the snake hadn't gotten to her first?"

"Oh!" Frankie grabbed my hand. "Speaking of psychics." She turned to Jack. "I'll be right back. I've got to show Darwin somethin'."

I groaned inwardly. *Bad timing, Frankie.* "Guess I'll be back," I said to Mallory right before I was being pulled through the crowd to the steps leading us onto the stage.

"This guy is amazing. He gave me a message from my great Aunt Violet earlier tonight, something only she would have known." Her voice rose in excitement as she led me to a temporary black curtain set up on the right of the stage. A line of costume-clad partygoers had formed in front of it. She patted my arm as we took our place at the end of the line. "Trust me, he's worth the wait."

A psychic? Huh. I wondered if he was the real deal. Guess I'd find out. We sipped our Halloweeny cocktails and I filled her in on Mallory's visit as we waited.

"That's good that she's tryin' to get over you leaving Savannah, right?" Frankie said. "Mend fences and all that?"

I nodded. "Yeah, sure." I couldn't tell her the real reason Mallory had come was because our father had visited her in a dream and had warned her I was going to be in danger.

"Well, she seems like a real sweet girl," Frankie said. "Though, I would have never known you gals were sisters. Besides the Georgia accents you really are nothing alike."

"I know. We're yin and yang." Fire and water. Literally. Which is what makes our magick so strong together. Logically, we should cancel each other out, weaken each other, but we don't. We complete each other like two sides of a coin. Grandma Winters says it has something to do with the dynamics of human love, that love has a magic all its own. But, even she doesn't seem to understand that part of it.

A woman-zombie appeared from behind the curtain, wiping at her eyes with a cocktail napkin. We all watched her find her group of zombie friends and give an animated account of her reading.

"Told ya," Frankie said, clinking my glass with hers and grinning. "Landon sure knows how to throw a party."

When it was my turn, I handed my drink to Frankie to hold and stepped behind the curtain.

Our eyes met and my heart almost stopped. "You!"

Zach Faraday leaned back in his chair, dark eyes shining, a small smile tugging at the corner of his mouth. "Have a seat."

I should have known. I forced my legs to move me forward, trying not to show how nervous he made me. *Breathe, Darwin.* I slid into the seat and tried to smile. "Zach, right?"

"Yes, Darwin." He leaned toward me, resting his elbows on the table and turned his palms up. He wore a black knit short-sleeved shirt, and I was getting a good eye-full of his smooth, muscular arms. "Please, place your hands in mine."

I moved my attention back to his mouth. *He remembered my name?* That wasn't good. Remaining invisible to this man seemed like the smarter thing to do. Too late. I wiped my damp palms on my tights before lifting them. *I could just get up and leave. No one was forcing me to do this.* I almost got the nerve to leave but then I made the mistake of looking up into his eyes. They pulled me in like magnets. Commanding. Lethal. I would obey.

I felt my hands shake as I rested them in his large palms. A vibration began immediately as he closed his hands around mine. It traveled through my body, making me hyper aware of our connection. I could suddenly feel his heartbeat through my palms, hear his slow deep exhales, and smell the pheromones on his breath. Everything else fell away. Our eyes were locked and I lost all sense of time. For the first time in my life I truly felt powerless.

My eyes moved to his mouth as he began to speak in a low, husky voice. "I knew you were a hybrid, like me." He smiled and leaned over the table, pulling me closer to him. His mouth stopped by my ear and a jolt of energy made me feel like I was falling off a cliff as his warm breath touched my face. "I see water. Your element, yes?"

"Yes," I whispered, closing my eyes to the assault of emotions he was conjuring up. *Heavens, why did I just admit that so easily?*

"I see your father."

My father? My eyes popped open. He leaned back just enough to let our gaze meet. Unfortunately we were only inches apart now. My head was swimming. His eyes gleamed like black onyx as he made a little tsk, tsk sound.

"He's trapped. Held prisoner, but it is by his own doing. He broke the rules. Magick and mortals are forbidden to mix in this dimension. There are consequences."

My heart felt like a tire that was being pumped up to the point of exploding. How did he know this? He moved his mouth closer to mine, holding my eyes. "He broke the code by falling in love." He was so close now, his breath warmed my lips. My whole body trembled. "A noble reason. Love."

It took all the strength in my being to pull away from this man. But, I managed to fight enough to put a few inches between us and slide my hands from his heated grip. The shaking slowed to a slight tremble as he frowned, watching me. My whole world felt exposed suddenly. Like a veil had been ripped open. My secret, my family's secret, was no longer safe. I had to get out of there. I might as well be standing in front of him naked.

I moved my chair back, watching him warily.

"Wait, Darwin." His eyes dimmed, the sparks subsiding. "There's something else. You need to be careful. There's danger in your future. And I think..." His head tilted as if he were listening to something far off. "I think we will face it together."

Now, that did scare me. "Okay." I stood up, willing my legs to hold me. "Thank you. I'll..." I backed up. "I'll keep that in mind." I backed around the corner and almost stumbled into Frankie's arms.

"Hey, sugar, you okay?" Frankie asked. "You're trembling. Pretty intense, huh?"

"Yeah." I breathed, taking my drink from her hand and downing it. *Danger? Face it together? No way! I was going to stay as far away from that man as humanly possible.*

She half-smiled, still looking worried. "Better?"

"Better." I nodded, still aware of the energy drain. Now I just felt weak.

We made our way back down the stage stairs and into the party crowd. I still felt Zach with me, his presence stuck in my mind like a burning ember. I was so confused. I just wanted to not think about him. To go back in time and never meet him. Tears pricked my eyes. *How did he know about my father?*

We reached Mallory, who was in a conversation with a young blond guy dressed like a fireman. Now that was poetic.

"Hey, Mal," I said. "Frankie and I are going to go get a refill." I shook my empty glass.

Her smile faded as she looked at me. "You all right? You're white as a ghost."

"Yeah, I'll fill you in later." I gave her a hug which deepened her frown. "Later," I assured her.

At the bar, we waited in line behind a man dressed as a pirate, complete with a real live parrot on his shoulder. He looked familiar, but I couldn't quite place him. He was chatting with another man wearing a red shirt that said "Devil". *Not a very original costume.*

As I talked with Frankie, I kept glancing at the pirate. He seemed so familiar. *Had he come into the pet boutique?* I tried to place him with a pet other than the parrot.

The parrot tilted its head and sidestepped down the pirate's arm. With a graceful hop, it landed on my forearm. I made a little yip sound, startled by the sudden vision of a snake. Just a small jolt of energy accompanied it, so I shook my other arm frantically to dissipate it.

Frankie laughed as the parrot reached for the cherry on the end of the plastic stick in my cup. The snake vision helped me remember where I had seen this man. "Duncan, right?" I said aloud. "The trapper?"

He turned around, saw his parrot on my arm and grinned. "In the flesh. Peaches, where are your manners?" He held his hand under the bird's belly and it stepped onto it, my cherry in its beak. "Sorry, sugar, not very good with faces and I think I'd remember you. Have we met?"

"Oh, well, not officially. I'm Darwin Winters. I was there the night you got that rattlesnake out of Rose Faraday's condo."

"Oh, right." He shook his head slowly. "Poor woman, very unfortunate for her. You look different in that cat costume." He eyed me appreciatively and motioned to his friend. "This here's my buddy McGillis. He actually ended up with her."

"Her?" I asked.

"The rattler."

"Oh!" I turned my attention to McGillis. "So, like as a pet?"

"More as an educating the public thing. Me and my partner, Sammy Harris, we opened up the Serpentarium over on 6th Street. Got over thirty poisonous species in there right now. You should come by."

Over thirty poisonous snakes in one place? I shivered and forced a smile. "Sure." *Walk right into a big den of snakes. On purpose. Who wouldn't think that was a good idea?*

While Frankie was introducing herself to the guys, I decided I should befriend these two, since I was trying to solve a murder with a poisonous snake as the weapon of choice.

"So, this snake place, is it open to the public?" I asked McGillis.

"Yep, Friday and Saturday from 9 a.m. to 9 p.m. Saturday nights get pretty busy."

"Guess I can check it out next Saturday." I turned to Frankie and smiled. "You up for coming with me?"

She shook her head. "Sorry, darlin'. Not too fond of snakes. Saw my share of 'em at Pirate City."

I nodded my understanding. Pirate City was St. Pete's local homeless camp. Frankie lived there before she won the lottery a few years back. I'd get Mallory to go with me. She wasn't afraid of much. Might have to bribe her, though.

* * *

The party didn't start winding down until three in the morning. Mallory and I collapsed at a table with Landon, Sylvia, Frankie and Jack. Parts and pieces of our costumes were piled up in front of us, and we had switched to water and finger sandwiches as we chatted, tired and happy.

I stroked Mage, Landon's black shepherd, who had left Landon's feet to rest his head in my lap. I cringed at first, but no visions came so I happily gave him whatever attention he wanted. My ears perked up when I heard Frankie pumping Landon for more information about Zach.

"Zach Faraday?" Landon picked up a sandwich triangle. "I've known him for a few years. Just ran into him last week and got him to agree to be the entertainment tonight. Guess he's back in town for his mother's funeral. I'm surprised he came back, actually, considering he and his mother weren't on speaking terms. Seems to really impress people with his psychic ability." He took a bite and chewed. "What'd you think of him?"

Mallory stiffened beside me at the mention of Zach's name and glanced at me, her eyes wide. I nodded. Well, at least he didn't live here in St. Pete. Now that the funeral was over, he'd probably go back to wherever he came from. That wouldn't be soon enough for me.

Then Landon's words hit me. *Wait, he and his mom weren't speaking? They must have really had a falling out. Was it bad enough that he could have been the one that slipped the rattlesnake into her condo? Is he dangerous enough to murder his own mother?*

"Oh, I thought he was amazing. No way could he fake what he told me," Frankie said. Her wig looked like road kill on the table in front of her. Her cropped red hair stuck up on her head. "I really believe he was communicating with my great aunt Violet."

Sylvia was shaking her head. "Not good. People should not mess with the spirits."

Forget spirits. Living people were the dangerous ones.

"I don't see what the harm is. If all they want to do is get a message to their loved ones that they're okay, what's wrong with that?" Jack asked.

"How do you know it's really your loved one? Could be a deceiving spirit just trying to turn you away from God." Sylvia made a sign of the cross over her chest. "Is not for us to mess with."

"Oh, I don't know, Sylvia," Mallory spoke up. "Don't you think that if someone had a gift, like being a psychic, that gift came from God and He would want the person to use it?"

"No," Sylvia said emphatically. "Is only trouble."

I could see Mallory's disappointment in that answer. She could deny caring what other people thought all she wanted. I knew deep down it bothered her, too.

"Well, I think there are lots of things we just can't fathom with our limited human brains," Landon said. He turned to me. "You've been awfully quiet, Darwin. What did you think of our party psychic?"

"He seemed to shake you up good, darlin'," Frankie said. "You never did tell me why."

Mallory stared at me. I could feel the anxiety wafting from her.

"He, um... knew some things about my father." I felt Mallory's anxiety jump up to a new level. "I think he's the real deal. Kind of scary. And on that note, I think it's time I get my little sister home."

CHAPTER THIRTEEN

Monday, we officially started Mallory's training to help in the boutique. I figured since she was going to be around for awhile, I'd keep her busy and out of trouble. Plus, she really was good with the customers. She was in her element helping the dog owners pick out costumes for the annual Dog-O-Ween contest coming up. One problem solved. On to the next.

We took a cab Saturday morning to McGillis's Serpentarium. Mallory stared out the window, scowling, her arms crossed over my favorite turquoise silk shirt. My bribe to get her to come.

"It won't be that bad." I paid the cab fare and we stepped out, staring up at the large 3-D metal cobra draped around the entrance.

I adjusted my straw bag and straightened my shoulders. "Come on. That's the biggest one we'll see today."

"It better be," Mallory whispered.

We paid the guy at the window and stepped through the door. The air inside the building was warm and moist. The lighting was dim. The smell was not pleasant. Rows and rows of glass cages lined the room. In the middle of the room sat tables with displays of skeletons, papery skins and laminated information about the reptiles.

I walked cautiously to the first glass cage to my right and peered in. Curled up on the pebbles and straw was a mass of light brownish muscle with beady black eyes. I read the sign on its cage.

"The King Cobra is the largest venomous snake in the world." Yikes. I glanced at him. "Well, hello there largest venomous snake in the world. So glad you're behind that glass." I fought a shiver.

"He's kind of cute." Mallory pressed her face closer to the glass. "Hey, big guy. It's gotta be boring in there for you."

"I'm not sure snakes can get bored." Though, who knows? Maybe they do. I moved to the next cage, leaving Mallory to her conversation. "Wow, hey, Mal, check this guy out." I scooted over to make room for her. We stared at the slim snake decorated with red, yellow and black bands of color.

"You're a pretty one," Mallory said, leaning down to get closer. "Must be a girl."

I glanced at the sign. "Eastern Coral Snake. Reclusive, has to literary chew on you to inject venom."

Mallory laughed. "Poor thing. It needs longer fangs." She moved on to the next cage.

I glanced around. *What was that noise?* It sounded like someone had turned on a sprinkler. I crossed the room and peered into the cages. Some of the snakes were very active, bobbing around and pressing themselves against the glass. They were all stunning in their own way.

Ah, there was the source of the noise. I stepped closer, feeling just a bit uncomfortable as I stared the large rattlesnake in the eye. It was coiled up, a pile of brown scaly muscle, the end of its tail shimmying in warning.

"That's her," a male voice said behind me.

I jumped a little and turned. "Oh, hey, McGillis. Startled me. I didn't hear you come in. This is her? Oh, the snake that killed Rose Faraday?"

He had his hands resting on narrow hips, an appreciative smile on his face. "Yep. She's a bugger, too."

Mallory joined us. "So, this is the murderess."

I shot her a look. "She was just doing what comes naturally to snakes. Following her instincts." I pictured the man-sized shadow creeping up to the lanai from the vision. *Yeah, he or she was the one responsible for Rose's death. Not this stunning creature behind the glass. How was I going to find out who that person was?*

"So, McGillis, I know that these snakes are native to Florida but do people also keep them as pets?"

"Well, not pets *per se*. But there are currently five people in St. Pete that have class three licenses to own venomous reptiles."

"Do you think this snake could have..." I chose my wording carefully, "escaped from one of those people and ended up in Rose's living room?"

He stared at the snake for a moment. "I suppose it's possible. That would explain her close proximity to civilization. They're pretty shy and tend to stay away from people. But we are

acquainted with all the herps in the area and I
don't recall any of 'em keeping a rattler. Besides, if
she was a pet, she should have been microchipped.
It's the law."

"Herps?"

"Herpetologists. People who are into reptiles."

"Oh." I nodded and wiped at my brow with the
back of my hand. Boy, it was warm in here. "Is
there a public record of those licenses?"

"Everything is a matter of public record
nowadays." His eyes darkened and then he forced
a smile. "Hey, do you want to watch a feeding?"

"What do y'all feed them?" Mallory asked, a
touch of panic in her voice.

"Nothin' live, don't worry," he chuckled.
"Frozen rats or mice."

My stomach clenched. Even if they weren't live,
I didn't want to see a feeding. Thank heavens the
door opened and another man sauntered in. I
heard Mallory make a noise deep in her throat.

This man stood in stark contrast to McGillis's
Bermuda shorts and sleeveless t-shirt. Mid-thirties
and tanned, he wore khaki pants and a pink polo
shirt, his sandy blond hair cut stylishly. He oozed
confidence and charm.

"Hey, Sammy." McGillis waved him over and
introduced us. "This here's Darwin and Mallory
Winters."

"Nice to meet you." Sammy shook our hand,
holding Mallory's hand longer than necessary. I
noticed she didn't mind a bit. "You ladies don't
strike me as the reptile type." His tone was teasing,
but his eyes were sharp.

Funny, he did strike me as the reptile type. The way his hooded eyes were glued to my little sister. I looked back at the rattlesnake. She was less intimidating. At least she was behind glass.

"Hey Sammy, any of the guys keep a rattler that you know of? Jamison maybe?"

"Last time we talked, he was planning on acquiring some." He put the word *acquiring* in air quotes. "Why? What's up?"

I snuck a glance at Sammy. His attention was still completely on my sister. I wanted to throw my body between them. I shifted my glance to McGillis. I also nudged Mallory and when she turned to me, I shook my head in warning. She was staring back at Sammy like it was her feeding time. I didn't like this at all. Mallory had never even been on a date. This guy had probably dated every girl on the planet.

"Well, Darwin here thought maybe this gal was being kept and escaped. That would explain how she was so close to a populated area."

I would have preferred McGillis not throw my theory out there for the world to hear. Wouldn't want it getting back to the killer that I was suspicious. *Thanks for throwing me under the bus, McGillis.*

Sammy just shrugged. "I can ask him if he lost one next time we talk."

"Just a thought," I mumbled. Thank heavens a group of boy scouts came in the door at that moment. Their energy and voices were a welcome interruption. "Well, thank y'all for the tour." I grabbed Mallory's elbow. "We'll get out of your hair now."

"See y'all later." Mallory waved, smiling at Sammy as I pulled her through the door.

"Hope so." Sammy threw a thousand watt smile back at her.

"No, Mal." I pulled out my cell phone to call a cab but kept walking to put some distance between us and the snakes, especially the human one.

"What?" There was more than a little irritation in her tone.

"He's too old for you, and too slick." I asked for a cab and then sat down on a bench.

Mallory plopped down beside me, her face flushed with irritation and probably a rush of hormones. "He was hot. You need to stop being so overprotective. I'm an adult now, you know."

"Barely." I sighed.

"And why do you think he's slick anyway?" She scowled at me as she said the word 'slick'. "We've only known him for like five seconds. You're such a hypocrite, Darwin." She crossed her arms and stared out at the cars going by. "You don't want people judging you but you judge someone after five seconds."

Wow. This guy really got to her. I knew Mallory well enough to know I had to back off. The more I protested the more determined she was going to be. "All right." I took a deep breath and let the negative energy go with a long exhale. "You're right. I shouldn't be so judgmental. But you know I just don't want you getting hurt."

She made a little half laugh sound, which was her white flag. "You don't want me to have any fun." She turned and grinned at me. Her green eyes practically glowed in the sunlight.

"Yep, that's it. I'm the fun police."

CHAPTER FOURTEEN

Wednesday afternoon I sat at a small table beneath Cassis's olive colored umbrellas, waiting for Will. With his work schedule, we had to sneak in time together whenever we could and Mallory had enough of a handle on the boutique now that I didn't feel guilty about taking a lunch.

A cold front had brought in cooler weather so I sipped a hot tea while I waited. A shadow soon stood over me and, smiling, I turned to greet Will. Only it wasn't Will.

"Dining alone?" Zach Faraday asked. His eyes were masked by dark sunglasses.

I turned away from him, ignoring my traitorous heartbeat. "Waiting for a friend." *Please go away. Pretty please with sugar on top.*

No such luck. He came around and took the seat across the table from me.

He slid his glasses off, and we stared at each other for longer than I was comfortable with. I folded my arms finally. "Is there somethin' I can help you with, Mr. Faraday?"

His eyes darkened and I felt a rush of scalding air blow through me. "Yes. Actually there is." He leaned back in the chair and folded his hands. "You were the reason the police came to discover my mother's body."

I blinked. This didn't sound like a question. More like an accusation.

"Okay," I said. *What else did he expect me to say?* I pulled my sweater tighter around me. "And?"

"Can you take me through how that night unfolded?"

I stared at him over my teacup. *What was he after? Surely, the police gave him all the information about that night?* Finally I shrugged. No harm in telling him, I guess. After all, it was his mother. Maybe Landon was wrong about Zach's and his mother's relationship? Maybe they were close.

"All right. My sister and I were on one of those walking ghost tours and found Lucky in the Traveler's Palm Inn conference room. Actually, she kinda jumped on my sister and held on for dear life. She seemed really traumatized so we decided to find her owner. Not that tough, since your mother's address was on her collar." Okay, so I was leaving out the vision with the shadow person. He wouldn't have believed me anyway. "We knocked, but there was no answer so we went around back. The lanai screen was ripped and a broken potted plant lay busted on the tile. Seemed odd so I called my detective friend. He didn't think anything was suspicious until he talked to the neighbors and no one had seen your mother for a few days. Plus the next door neighbor mentioned an odor. That, along with Lucky normally being an indoor cat, well... he decided to call for back up and enter the condo. Where they found your mother."

I glanced around. *Where the heck was Will?*

"And the snake that bit her, it was still in her home?"

"Yes." I snuck a glance at him while he stared out at the backed up traffic on Beach Drive. Why did he make me so uncomfortable? It was like watching a volcano, all hard rock on the outside, bubbling molten lava beneath the surface ready to erupt at any moment. Was he suspicious of her death, too? "I'm sorry for your loss. Were you and your mother very close?"

His jaw twitched and he brought his intense gaze back to me. "We hadn't spoken in awhile. I'm out of town a lot." His eyes dropped and he sighed. "You know how it is. Two different worlds. Makes it hard to communicate."

I blinked. *Two different worlds? Was he talking about my father again?* His confiding tone threw me for a loop.

He continued quietly, almost like he was talking to himself. "My mother, she was a nineteen-year-old gypsy when my father found her. She became his prisoner. Unlike your father, mine didn't break the rules for love. He wasn't that noble." His eyes flashed and then cooled as he smiled at me. "I always reminded her too much of my father."

Okay. Wow. I was really starting to feel in over my head here. I didn't want to know this much about him. Unfortunately, I couldn't stop myself or my curious nature. "Um, so that's why you two didn't speak?"

"Yes." He shrugged. "She was a very stubborn woman. Viciously so at times."

He was being so open here, I had to ask. "Zach, do you know of anyone that might have wanted to harm your mother?"

His attention was fully on me now. He tilted his head slightly and leaned forward. In the bright afternoon sun, I could see flecks of red glinting in his dark eye. They were mesmerizing. "You are suspicious of her death?"

I swallowed. "Yes." There I go, telling him the truth again. I began to panic. Now he was going to ask why I was suspicious. Luckily, Will approached the table at that moment.

I'm sure my relief was apparent as I sank back in the chair and let Will greet me with a kiss on the cheek.

Will stared at Zach and then back at me. "Sorry I'm late. Got tied up."

"Well, here, I'm being rude." Zach nodded at me as he stood and held out a hand. "Zachary Faraday."

"Zach is Rose's son," I offered, as Will shook his hand and eyed him suspiciously. "We met at her funeral service."

"Detective Blake. So sorry for your loss."

He and Zach continued to stare at each other for a moment. Finally Zach's face broke into a dazzling smile and he chuckled. It was the first time I had ever seen him really smile. "You two kids enjoy your lunch. Darwin, can we continue this conversation at a later date?"

"Sure." I cringed inwardly at his use of the word *date*. "Oh wait, Zach!" He turned back to me. "Do you know who Lucky's vet was? I need to make sure she's not due for any shots."

"No, but I can find that information for you. I'll be in touch."

"Interesting character," Will said, watching Zach make his way across the road through the traffic. "What else did you two have to talk about besides the cat?"

Was he jealous? I held my hands over the steaming cup of tea, suddenly aware of the warmth that had left with Zach. "He wanted to know about the night we found his mother's body. I guess he's still trying to deal with his grief. Figure out some rhyme or reason for such a tragedy." I picked up the menu and changed the subject.

I hated keeping things from Will and that's all I seemed to do since we met, but there was nothing else I could tell him about Zach. I certainly couldn't tell him that Zach saw danger in my future. Or that I'd be facing it with him. I shivered. "I think today calls for some warm French onion soup." *Comfort food.*

"Cold?" Will slid his chair around next to mine and wrapped an arm around me. "That better?"

I grinned up at him as he pressed his lips into my hair. "You know what would be even better?" His slow smile made my insides hum. I smacked him playfully on the arm and scooted my chair sideways a bit so I could face him. "What would be even better is if you told me something about your family. You know, since you've had the pleasure of meeting my sister."

He ran his fingers up my arm. An echo of sadness washed over me.

"All right." He cleared his throat. "I had an older brother, Christopher. He was ten years my senior. When I was eleven, he was murdered. Stabbed to death at a party. No one was ever convicted. My mother died a year later from the grief and stress. She never recovered from losing him."

I entwined my fingers with his. How awful. I couldn't imagine losing one of my sisters that way. I could see why he never talked about his family now. "And your father?"

"He lives in Tampa. He's almost seventy now. He hasn't been the same since losing my mom. Still talks about her to anyone that'll listen." He shrugged. "He's adapted, though. Learned how to microwave dinners and all that."

"I'm so sorry, Will." I shifted to rest my head on his shoulder. "Is that why you became a homicide detective?"

He laughed and then shrugged, kissing the top of my head. "Yeah. I guess I wanted to solve all the unsolved crimes. So no family would have to feel like we did. No closure, no justice. It leaves an open wound."

"But, you can't solve them all."

"No." His voice rumbled close to my ear. "But I can sure try."

I snuggled closer to him as we waited for our food. An odd mixture of sadness and frustration gripped me. I could help him solve some of the more unsolvable crimes. If only I could confide in him about what I knew. Oh and that I was once again investigating a murder behind his back.

CHAPTER FIFTEEN

McGillis had said there were five people in St. Pete with a license to keep venomous snakes. Fortunately, Florida's Fish and Wildlife Commission made its database of those licenses public record. A quick internet search gave me the five addresses.

I was on my own Saturday. Sylvia and I had decided to keep Darwin's Pet Boutique open on Saturdays during the heavy tourist season to make up for the slower summer sales. Mallory had agreed to work that Saturday and let me check out the snake owners.

The first house on the list sat about five miles north of downtown. It was a bit of a shock when the cab pulled up to a typical Florida neighborhood with older ranch houses. I was expecting something more secluded. More sinister. I wondered if the neighbors were aware of the dangerous snakes inside.

I asked the cabbie to wait for me and made my way up the driveway to the front door.

Within a few seconds a small girl, her wispy hair in two uneven ponytails, answered the door.

"Hi." I smiled down at her. She held a red Popsicle and it was dripping down her chubby arm. *Did I have the right house? Surely, this cute little girl wasn't living with dangerous snakes?* "Is your mom or dad home, sweetie?"

A woman walked up behind her, wiping her wet hands on a dishtowel. "Hannah, what have I told you about opening this door?" she scolded. "Go eat that at the table."

She eyed me suspiciously. "Hi, we don't want any magazines."

"Oh, no," I said, smiling. "I'm not a salesperson. I just wanted to ask you a question."

She glanced behind her and folded her arms. "All right?"

"Were you or anyone in your residence acquainted with Rose Faraday?"

Her mouth twisted in thought. "No, can't say I recognize the name. Who is she?"

"She was a local psychic that got bit by a rattler and passed away last week. I'm just following up with the people who own venomous snakes in the area to see if they might have information on where the rattlesnake came from."

The woman's face registered genuine sadness. "That's awful. Well, my boyfriend keeps two Burmese pythons here but no rattlers. Aren't they native in the wild?"

"In the wild, yes. But she was bitten in her condo."

"Huh." The woman shook her head. "A psychic you said? Shouldn't she have seen that coming?"

"Guess even psychics can't see everything coming." I shrugged. "Well, thank you for your time." I went back to the cab, gave him the second address and mentally crossed this house off my list.

The second house was a nice brick rancher with a chain across the gravel drive, a 'No Trespassing' sign swinging from the chain. The cabbie pulled over to the side of the road and I walked around the chain, noticing JAMISON painted on the black mailbox. This must be the guy Sammy said recently acquired two rattlesnakes. My heart sank as I stood there ringing the bell and knocking and no one came to the door. Rats. I'd have to come back. I definitely needed to talk to Mr. Jamison. Right now he'd stay on the list.

I was starting to feel a bit queasy as we headed west through stop-and-go traffic. I guess I just wasn't used to being in a car. Even with the air conditioning blasting from the front vents, the air felt stale and suffocating.

When we stopped at the third house, I stumbled out of the back seat and sucked in fresh air. There was a rusty pick-up truck parked in the front yard's scrubby brown grass. After my stomach settled down, I approached the front door.

Before I could knock, a large man holding a beer can greeted me through the screen.

"You lost, sweet thing?" He opened the screen and a whiff of stale beer and urine made my stomach clench again.

"Just had a question for you, sir." Had to do this quick and skedaddle. "You own poisonous snakes, correct?"

He leered at me through glassy eyes. "You came here to take a gander at my snake? Well, come on in."

I ignored him and my sudden urge to run back to the taxi. I did however glance behind me to make sure the taxi was still there. "Were you acquainted with a woman named Rose Faraday?"

His face hardened. "Is she that stripper bitch? I done told the police I didn't grab her, she was fallin' off the stage and I just kept her from fallin'."

I blinked. Wow. Time to go. He obviously wasn't the murderer. I doubt he could sneak around at night without falling into a lake or getting hit by a bus. "No. That's not her. Thank you for your time." I sang "la la la la la" in my head to drown out his parting comments as I hurried back to the taxi and slammed the door. "Go, please!"

By the time we reached the fifth and final house, I was feeling really nauseous and frustrated. This was looking more and more like a waste of valuable time.

We drove back down 18th Street toward the Bay and crossed back over Beach Drive. I sat up as the driver pulled over in front of a black gated driveway leading up to a peach stucco mansion. "This is it." *Now this was different.*

"Just wait here, please." I instructed the driver before getting out and approaching the gate. There was a black call box on the right side. I mashed the button.

A female voice erupted from the box. "Yes? Can I help you?"

"Hi," I waved in case she could see me. "My name is Darwin Winters. I'm not selling anything. I just have a question to ask about a woman named Rose Faraday. I'm trying to find someone who knew her."

After a beat, the woman answered. "I'm sorry. Mr. Grayson not home until Wednesday. You come back."

I squinted at the monstrous house. She must be the housekeeper or caretaker. Surely she knows everything that goes on in that house then. "The name doesn't ring a bell for you?"

"No, Miss Winters," the box squawked. "You come back."

I sighed. "Okay. Well, thanks for your time." Nothing. Zero. Zilch. I fell back in the taxi, my stomach now growling, my head foggy with frustration. Time to head home.

CHAPTER SIXTEEN

I tried to keep busy while Mallory relaxed on the balcony Sunday morning with Lucky curled up in her lap, watching the activity across the street at Straub Park. Today was the annual Dog-O-Ween costume contest. St. Pete vibrated with the excitement of it all. Above the bird calls and rustling of the breeze in the palm trees, voices and laughter reached us. A temporary stage was being erected, orange lights were being strung in the trees, and vendors were setting up booths to sell food and drinks. The weather was to die for. Sunny with a light breeze. It was going to be a great time, so why was I feeling so down?

Mallory must have heard my sigh. "All right, spill it. Is it Will?"

I looked up from clipping some purple and yellow pansies into a bowl of water for new flower essence. Mallory and Lucky were both staring at me.

"No." I shrugged, removing my straw sunhat and tossing it by the French doors. "Yes. I don't know." I slipped the tiny sheers back into my gardening apron. I shouldn't be handling the flowers while feeling down anyway. My vibrations were all wrong.

Mallory frowned at me. "You're really hooked on him, huh?"

I took a seat beside her and stroked Lucky's silky, black fur. "Yeah, I think I am." Lucky gave me an approving meow that sounded more like a bird chirp. I smiled. "Glad to see you're warming up to me, girl. Must be the tuna therapy."

Mallory took a deep breath and blew it out loudly. "Well, it's obvious he's crazy about you, too, so I don't know why you don't just come clean with him."

I glanced at her. I didn't really want to get into this conversation with Mallory. It would just lead to her getting angry about me being ashamed of our family. Again. I opted for being diplomatic instead. "Maybe you're right." And then used the avoidance technique. "Oh, sugar. I've gotta check on the pumpkin treats in the oven. Be right back."

I stood in front of the oven, the timer showing four more minutes. Moving around to the front of the kitchen bar, I fussed with the large basket we were donating to the winner of the dog costume contest. Rearranging the contents, I placed the hundred dollar gift certificate on top. The skull shaped pumpkin treats would be the last thing to go in there and then I could wrap it all up in cellophane.

With a jolt, I suddenly realized my thoughts had drifted off to Zach Faraday and his warning that I would be in danger. Why did everyone suddenly think I was in danger? It was irritating. I shuddered and pushed the thoughts away. Filling my mind instead with Will; his smile, the kindness in his blue eyes, his shoulders, his laugh—

The oven timer buzzed at the same time Lucky leaped onto the counter beside me from Mallory's arms. I jumped. "Jeeze O Pete!"

Mallory laughed as she pulled her hair up in a hair tie. "You really need to relax, Sis. Stress isn't good for you." Mallory ignored the childish gesture of me sticking my tongue out at her and sauntered into the kitchen to turn off the oven timer. "You want these treats out?" she called.

"Yes. Thank you." I plopped onto the stool and scratched Lucky behind the ear. She leaned into my hand. "She's right, you know. You could give me a little more to go on besides a person in black. Surely, you saw more than that? I mean, I am giving you free room and board, and thinking about buying stock in tuna."

Lucky stuck her butt up in the air and her face in the basket.

"Hey, nosey, be careful." Mallory plucked Lucky off the counter. "Darwin might just stick a bow on you and add you to that basket." She rubbed her nose in Lucky's fur and then stretched the cat over her shoulder.

I smiled. She was attached to Lucky already. Good. It wouldn't take too much convincing to get Mallory to take her back to Savannah with her. If and when she went back home. I needed to figure out who put that rattler in Rose's condo before I had a permanent roommate.

* * *

Mallory and I moseyed across Beach Drive into Straub Park around noon. Cars were parked on both sides of the street. I scanned the crowd above the big winner's basket in my arms. Spotting Frankie and Sylvia standing in front of the stage chatting with a short, balding man in a bright orange shirt, I nudged Mallory. "Over there."

"*Olá donas!*" Sylvia flashed her larger than life smile at us from beneath a large black sunhat and dark glasses. "Beautiful day, no?"

"Perfect." I greeted her with an air kiss. "Hey, Frankie."

"Hi, Darwin. Hi, Mallory." Frankie grinned at my sister and hugged me. "I want you to meet Edward Goodchild, the director of events for our Humane Society. They sponsored the party this year and all the vendors here are donating a percentage of their profits to the Humane Society." As I adjusted the basket and shook his hand, Frankie continued, "This is my good friend, Darwin Winters, and her sister, Mallory, who's visiting us from Savannah. Darwin co-owns Darwin's Pet Boutique with Sylvia." She pointed to our boutique across the street.

"So nice to meet you, ladies." Edward's soft voice matched his baby blue eyes. "Thank you for donating the first place prize. We're so excited. We've got over eighty pets registered for the contest so far."

"Our pleasure. It's a worthy cause." I motioned to the basket. "Where would you like me to put this?"

"Oh, just under the judges table would be fine. Thank you."

"Okay. Well, we're going to go check out the vendors. Y'all are the judges?" I asked.

Sylvia and Edward nodded.

"Yep," Frankie chuckled. Disqualified me from entering Itty and Bitty in the contest, but didn't stop me from dressin' them up. Be right back," she said, placing a hand on Edward's arm. "Come see my girls." We followed Frankie over to the dog stroller parked at the judges table and she unzipped the canopy.

A tiny devil and angel with Chihuahua faces peered up at us. The devil yipped. Frankie scooped her up and I scooped up the angel. "This is Bitty. The squeaky wheel." Frankie handed her to Mallory.

"Nice to meet you, Bitty," Mallory said, adjusting the tiny dog's devil horns. She held her up for a closer inspection. "You're about the cutest devil I've ever seen."

"And what pretty wings you have," I said, kissing Itty. Her tiny tongue licked my nose and then her ears went up. She spotted a golden retriever with three heads coming our way and started shaking. I turned so she couldn't see it. "Oh, poor thing."

"Yeah, they aren't too keen on the costumes." She took Bitty back from Mallory. "All right, gals, back in hiding for you two. I should've put you both in scaredy-cat costumes," she chuckled to herself.

I put Itty back, too and gave her an extra ear scratch. "See you in a bit, Frankie. We're going to go check out the vendors. You want anything?"

"Wouldn't mind a glass of cold white wine if you come across one." She glanced at her watch. "We've got about a half an hour before the judging starts."

"I'll see what I can do." I hugged her and led Mallory through the park, which was filling up fast with people leading their costumed dogs around. We stopped and chatted with some of our regular customers. Some of the owners were dressed up, too. Lots of compliments were being thrown around as the festivities got under way.

Mallory was craving BBQ and I found a booth offering veggie burgers, so we split up. I was watching a Great Dane, a saddle and stuffed monkey riding on his back, sniff a pug dressed as a taco, when a deep voice spoke in my ear.

"I have a favor to ask of you."

My jaw clenched. I crossed my arms and turned around. "Hello, Zach."

He didn't waste time with pleasantries. "I've been invited to a Masquerade Ball on Friday evening and I need you to attend it with me."

I raised my eyebrows, baffled. *Was he trying to ask me out on a date?* "Seriously? Is that how you ask a girl out where you're from? It's not very effective, I gotta tell you." I narrowed my eyes. "Where are you from anyway?"

He stared at me for a moment. "Nowhere you would be familiar with. Will you attend with me?"

"No I will not. But there's plenty of eligible women in this town who I'm sure would love to go to a party with you." I pointed behind him. "That blonde over there, with the vampire pit bull looks like your type."

It was his turn to raise an eyebrow. "I'm not looking for a woman. It has to be you." He moved in closer to me and lowered his voice. I felt my insides hum. Whatever power he held sent every cell in my body vibrating. "I was asking around about my mother's recent clients. One of them, a Bernard Grayson, sent me an invite to this Masquerade Ball, and I have no idea who he is or why I was suddenly invited."

I frowned. The name sounded familiar. I still didn't understand why he wanted me to go with him. "And this has what to do with me?"

"You are the only other person who thinks my mother's death is suspicious. Though I think you are not telling me why, I need you to help me figure out if this Bernard Grayson person was involved."

After I got over the shock of him believing me, I realized it was a nice feeling. Someone actually believing me. Still, I was about to turn him down again and then it hit me. "Wait! Is this the Mr. Grayson of the 18th Street peach mansion?"

"Yes." His eyes narrowed. "You know him?"

"No. But I do know that he has a permit to have poisonous snakes. I'm in."

"Thank you, Darwin."

I suddenly thought about Will. I'm sure he wouldn't approve of me spending an evening with

Zachary. "But, this is not a date. I'll meet you there. And I'm bringing my sister."

The corner of his mouth twitched. "Call it whatever you wish. I'll meet you at the gate at eight o'clock sharp." He glanced down at my flip flops and let his eyes run up my bare legs, shorts and t-shirt. "You do have something appropriate for a Masquerade Ball, don't you?"

"Of course," I said. After he nodded and walked away, I thought again about how he believed there was danger in my future. The only danger I could see right now was him. What if he realized I was suspicious of his mother's death and is just trying to throw me off, because he actually had something to do with it? I would have to be careful.

When Mallory found me, I was the next in line for my veggie burger.

"So, Mal, what exactly does a girl wear to a Masquerade Ball?"

***

Mallory and I found a place in the crowd milling about the stage. The costume judging had begun, and I had almost forgotten the whole Zach-Masquerade Ball thing when I felt an arm slide around my belly and pull me against a solid, warm chest. The smell of coconut and fresh rain filled my senses. I smiled.

"Surprised?" Will asked, kissing my ear.

"Pleasantly," I whispered back, turning to look up into his sky blue eyes. "Thought you had to work today?"

"We got an early break." He leaned down and brushed my lips with his. His warm breath sent shivers down my arms.

I handed him my plastic cup, half full of white wine. "Cheers to that, Detective." As he took a sip, his eyes stayed locked on mine. I could see the shades of darker longing, the white sparks of desire. The commotion of people clapping, the shouts and barks, the conversations rising and falling in the crowd, it all melted into the background.

I turned in his arms so I could face him and he pulled me closer, every inch of my thin frame pressed against him. The October sun was no match for the heat being generated by our bodies being so close. He reached down, without breaking eye contact, and pressed his lips to mine, gently at first and then I felt his hunger grow. I tasted the wine on his tongue, the heat from his breath. I pulled away reluctantly as Mallory cleared her throat beside us.

My face flushed as my sister rolled her eyes at us. We shared a smile before I turned my attention back to the costume contest.

"You may need this to cool off," Will whispered, handing me back the cup of wine and pressing his lips on the back of my neck.

We watched the rest of the contest like that, me leaning into Will, happily laughing and cheering for the costumed dogs being led across the stage, clapping at the end when the winners were announced. The Great Dane with the monkey riding his back got the first place basket.

"I don't know how they picked just one. They were all amazing," I said.

"*You're* amazing." Will kissed the tip of my nose. There was a new intensity in his stare. "I have a surprise for you."

"Ooo, I like surprises," I said, beaming.

"I managed to finagle this Friday and Saturday off, and I'd like us to go away for the weekend."

"Us? You and me?" My mind whirled. The weekend? That would mean spending the night together. Sleeping together? Well, there would be a whole new level of commitment. And guilt about hiding things from him. And then panic struck. *Friday night? Oh heavens, that was the night of the Masquerade Ball.*

"Um." I bit my lower lip. *How was I going to tell him that I had already committed to going to the Ball with Zach Faraday?* His smile was fading the longer I waited to answer. "That really sounds amazing, Will, but..."

His head dropped and he broke eye contact. My heart lurched. The last thing I wanted to do was hurt this man in any way. He'd already been burned by his ex-wife, and I was the first woman he had taken a chance on since then.

"It's just, I've already made a commitment for Friday night." I hoped that would be enough information for him, but no such luck.

"A commitment?" His eyebrows raised. "Can't you get out of it?"

And here I was, at the crossroads. I took a deep breath and decided on the truth. After all, I would have said yes to spending the weekend with him. If

I was getting in that deep, he deserved the truth. "Let's get out of the crowd."

We moved silently across the stretch of grass to a bench at the end of the park, where only a few people were walking their dogs. I could see the sparkling bay waters from there, a small comfort.

"Okay." I held both of Will's hands. "Here's the thing. I agreed to go to a Masquerade Ball Friday night with Zachary Faraday."

Will's eyes narrowed, his expression morphing from curious to confused. "A date? You agreed to a date?"

I tried to stop his conclusions. "No, it's not a date," I said quickly. "It's sort of an investigation. See, I think his mother, Rose, was... murdered."

Will pulled his hands from mine. His mouth tightened and his eyes burned with suspicion. Panic fluttered like butterfly wings in my heart. This felt like Mad Dog's death all over again. He didn't believe me that Mad Dog had been murdered either. I felt all the old doubts and walls rising.

"Rose Faraday died from a heart attack following a snake bite. You're telling me you believe she was murdered by the rattlesnake?" Will's body had stiffened, his voice was raw.

"Yes... no." My chest was tightening so my words held a touch of breathlessness. "By a person, who let the rattlesnake into her condo. And Zach believes me." I mentally smacked myself. That sounded like a dig at Will. "He asked me to the Ball only because he thinks the person holding it, Bernard Grayson, might have something to do with his mother's death. Mr. Grayson has a license to house poisonous snakes. It just seems like too much of a coincidence not to check out." I stopped. Will was leaning back on the bench, his gaze now trained on the park, his jaw tight.

"Will?" I shifted to try to get him to look at me. "Say something, please."

"All this time." He still wasn't looking at me. That wasn't a good sign. "When I asked you what you and Mr. Faraday had to talk about, you were discussing this? This theory that his mother was murdered, but you couldn't mention it to me?" He turned to me then and I almost choked on the betrayal swimming in his eyes. "A homicide detective."

"I was going to talk to you about it, Will. I swear, but I wanted to have some kind of evidence so you didn't just think I was crazy."

He worked his jaw back and forth, staring at me. "Okay, so if there's no evidence, why do you both think she was murdered?"

Oh heavens. I couldn't tell him about my visions. Not like this, when he was so angry with me already. My body sank with my heart. I could do nothing but stare at him helplessly.

He nodded, his head dropping. After a moment of silence, he rubbed his hands roughly on his jeans and stood. "I have to trust you, Darwin. Or this won't work. Have fun at the party with Mr. Faraday."

I watched him walk away, stunned that things had taken such a wrong turn in such a short amount of time. I wanted to run after him, hold on to him, beg him to understand. Instead, I stood and went to find my sister, my heart shattering in my chest.

CHAPTER SEVENTEEN

I had called the vintage shop we bought our Halloween costumes from and asked for the saleswoman's help in dressing for the Ball. She had assured us she could find something perfect for me and Mallory, and she had delivered.

We stepped out of the taxi in front of the 18th street mansion in our fabulous gowns. Mallory wore a red satin number which shimmered like rubies in the moonlight. I wore a pink feathery gown that made me feel like I was wearing a cloud. Her mask was black velvet with red sequins and a red feather, mine was white with diamonds and pink pearls. I felt like Cinderella. If only my Prince Charming were here.

"There's Mr. Tall, Dark and Scary." Mallory nodded at the gate. Sure enough, Zach stood there waiting for us, dressed in a black tux and holding a black mask in his clasped hands.

The closer we got, the stronger I felt the pulse of power he exuded. His eyes met mine and then he let them move down my gown, a soft smile curving his mouth. "You look beautiful, Darwin." He caught my eye again and I suppressed a shiver.

"Thanks," I mumbled.

He turned his gaze on Mallory and chuckled. "Red suits you. I feel sorry for the man that betrays a creature such as yourself." He held out both arms. I glanced at Mallory. She looked confused and wary. I wondered if he could sense her power, too.

"Mal, come on," I whispered, taking Zach's right arm. "We're his dates, remember? We have to at least act like we like him."

"Right," she sighed, finally slipping her hand into the crook of his elbow.

Zach handed his invite to the muscles-in-a-tux at the front gate. He glanced from me to Mallory and shot Zach a sly smile. I noticed the C-shaped scar on his left cheek that ran from his eyebrow to his mouth. Violence must play a big part in his life. "Have a nice evening, Mr. Faraday, ladies."

Zach led us down the tiki torch lined travertine pathway, through the jungle of tropical plants to the front door.

"Good evening," a plump, dark haired woman greeted us. I wondered if this was the woman I spoke to through the speakers? I detected the same accent. "Follow me, please." She led us through the marble entranceway, around a staircase more suited for a hotel and into a cavernous ballroom. "Music and dancing in here. Food and drinks out by the pool. Enjoy the party."

"Ready?" Zach slipped on his mask.

"As I'll ever be." I, too, slipped on my mask, adjusting it so I could see through the holes. "Try to stay out of trouble," I threw at Mallory before Zach led me deeper into the room.

Men in tuxes and women in gowns were milling about and dancing to the jazz band playing on the stage. A colossal gold and crystal chandelier hung suspended above us from a high, rounded ceiling. Tables huddled on one side of the room, adorned with crisp, white table clothes and crystal lamps. The lacquered hardwood floor sparkled from two mirrored disco balls slinging light around the room.

I glanced up at Zach. Behind the mask, he was scanning the room.

"Would you know Mr. Grayson if you saw him?" I asked.

"Yes, I looked him up on the internet so I would be sure to recognize him." Distracted, he slipped his hand in mine. The jolt of energy startled me. "I don't see him. Come on, let's dance."

Pulling me to the middle of the floor, he positioned my arms around his neck, and then slid his arms around my lower back. I was suddenly glad my gown had so many layers. I was sure the heat radiating off this man was capable of lighting my underwear on fire.

As he led me effortlessly around the ballroom, I could feel his frustration growing.

"What's wrong, Zach?"

He sighed and his hot, iron-scented breath warmed the side of my face. "I don't recognize anyone here."

"Kind of hard, with everyone wearing masks. We'll just have to ask around. Surely someone here can point out Mr. Grayson."

He lowered his eyes to meet mine. "That might raise suspicions. Admitting we don't know the host?" He held my eyes, pulling me in closer to him with barely a movement. "The mask suits you. Emphasizes your eyes. They're stunning. So blue in this light they're practically violet."

I blinked. *Yeah, and yours are like staring into a bonfire.* "Thanks," I said out loud, clearing my throat and trying to clear my head of the sudden woozy feeling coming over me. *Was he causing me to feel like this? Or was it the maddening spots of light from the disco balls?*

Zach lifted a hand off my back and cupped my cheek, letting his thumb run softly across my bottom lip. I froze as his eyes moved to my mouth. The woozy feeling escalated to floating. All sound and movement ceased to exist.

From far away, I heard my own voice. "Zach. No."

With a whoosh, the ballroom and inhabitants returned. Zach dropped his hand and broke eye contact. "Come on."

I was trembling as he led me off the floor. Confused and feeling way out of my league, I knew I couldn't let myself be that vulnerable around him again.

We found Mallory standing where we left her but with company.

"Hey." She waved at us, her eyes luminous behind the mask. "You remember Sammy Harris, Darwin? From the Serpentarium?"

"Of course, hi, Sammy." I groaned inwardly, plastering a smile on my face and introduced him to Zach. "This is Zach Faraday."

The two men shook hands and Sammy's eyes narrowed. "Faraday? Any relation to the woman killed by the rattlesnake?"

"Yes," Zach answered, clasping his hands in front of him. "She was my mother."

"Wow," Sammy shook his head, "sorry for your loss, man. Such a freak thing to happen."

"They actually have the snake that bit her at the Serpentarium," Mallory told Zach.

Heavens, Mallory! Don't tell him that. I tensed and shook my head at her. What if Zach wanted revenge? He could take it out on the poor snake.

"Really?" Zach's tone was sharp as a blade as he stared at Sammy. "Do you own the snake?"

"Well, we do now. We take in unwanted snakes. Use them to educate the public." Sammy turned his attention back to Mallory. "She's a wild one." I wasn't sure whether he was talking about the snake or my sister. I had to stop myself from digging a heel into his foot as they smiled at each other. "Of course, the girl we brought to the party tonight is a sweetheart. An albino boa named Marsha. Want to meet her?"

"Sure," Mallory said.

"No," I said at the same time, trying to give Mallory a warning look. She wasn't paying a bit of attention to me.

Sammy chose to ignore my answer and led my sister out of the ballroom on his arm. I pulled Zach after them.

We ended up at the back of the house on the pool deck beneath the lanai. Some of the guests were lounging and chatting on the blue and white striped patio furniture with their champagne glasses and plates of food. Some were standing around in small circles, laughing and talking. Everyone looked amazing and seemed to be having a good time, without a care in the world. Must be nice.

The breeze blowing off the Gulf felt good, cooling off the dampness around my hairline. The pool water was like balm on my frazzled nerves. We followed Sammy around the left curve of the pool. As I walked, the water rippled beside me. My eyes widened. *Oops!* I tapped into the part of my mind that had wandered. Concentrating, I smoothed the water out. Whew. The effort was like moving a rusty door. Mallory was right. I should be practicing. If only to keep control on my power.

A low chuckle came from Zach beside me.

"What?" I threw at him. I didn't appreciate his sense of humor.

He smiled knowingly and kept walking.

We came to the open patio with a shiny, silver outdoor kitchen and stone fireplace. There, surrounded by a group of partygoers snapping pictures, was McGillis—looking dapper in a black tux with satin lapels—his hair slicked back. He was positioning a large albino snake around a cringing woman's shoulders.

"Oh my, it's so heavy," the woman squealed. "Hurry up, David, take the photo!"

A robust man—his face red, his mask discarded—held up the camera and the flash lit up the duo. "Got the proof! Our daughter's not gonna believe you touched a snake."

"Okay, get it off!" She had her eyes squeezed shut.

McGillis chuckled. "You were very brave, Mrs. Rosen." He shook her hand and called out, "Who's next?"

I heard Sammy's voice behind me. "Mallory, go ahead, she's really harmless."

"Sure, why not." Mallory stepped past me and walked up next to McGillis. "I'll hold her."

"Brave girl," he said, grinning.

I watched as he wrapped the creamy boa with pale orange spots around my sister's bare shoulders, its tongue flicking the air in front of her. I leaned toward Sammy. "So, boas don't bite?"

"Well, they can. Unusual though," Sammy said, folding his arms and rocking back on his heels, as he watched Mallory. "Don't worry, they're non-venomous. They kill by squeezing their prey to death. Marsha's not big enough to take down your sister."

Well, that didn't make me feel any better. I was relieved when the pictures were taken and the snake was lifted off her without incident. My relief was short lived though as Mallory grabbed my hand and pulled me over to McGillis.

"Your turn," she said, holding me there despite my protests. "Come on, Sis. Live a little."

"She really is a sweetheart," McGillis chuckled, unwrapping the albino snake from his own neck and holding her above my shoulders. "Ready?"

"As I'll ever be," I sighed. A few clicks of a camera and then... *ZAP!*

This time, it wasn't an image, but a searing pain that shot through my stomach like a lightning bolt. I fought to stay upright as the weight of the snake, together with its recent trauma, about sent me doubling over and crashing to the floor.

"You all right, sweetheart?" McGillis was rushing to slide Marsha off my body. "You look like you're gonna pass out."

"Fine, just a muscle spasm," I said through clenched teeth, trying to breathe through the pain. I was too weak to dispel the energy myself so when a light bulb burst above us, Mallory finally understood what was happening and rushed in to move me away from the crowd.

Zach followed us to a corner of the lanai. "Darwin? Everything all right?"

Ignoring him, I glanced at Mallory, gasping and feeling the blood rush back into my head as the pain began to subside. I pressed a hand against my stomach through the layers of my gown. "I need you to find out anything you can about that snake. How long they've owned it. What they feed it. Anything and everything."

She nodded and glanced at Zach warily. "Find her a place to sit down." Then to me, "I'll be right back."

"What's going on?" Zach asked, searching my face. "Something happened with the snake. Tell me."

Before I could answer, a voice behind us interrupted. "Ah, Mr. Faraday."

Zach and I both turned. I felt Zach tense up beside me, and then he shook the man's offered hand. "Mr. Grayson."

"Please, call me Bernard."

So, this was Bernard Grayson? The man was over fifty but fit, his eyes an almost fluorescent blue in his tanned face. He held a champagne glass and cigar in one hand and offered me the other one. "And the lovely lady?"

I fought to stand straight as a wave of nausea made my stomach lurch again. "Darwin Winters. Beautiful home you have." The pain had dulled enough to allow me to force a smile.

Bernard's eyes narrowed as he stared at me. I had a feeling he didn't miss much. "Thank you. Come, you two look in need of a drink." We followed him over to the outdoor bar where he instructed the bartender to give us whatever we wanted. I opted for water as my stomach still felt queasy.

"This really is a great party, Mr... Bernard," Zach began as he sipped his martini. "But, I'm afraid I don't understand why I was given an invitation. Do we know each other?"

Bernard's eyes narrowed but his mouth stayed locked in a smile. "Your mother never mentioned me to you?"

Zach's shoulders moved slightly. "No. We weren't very close. Should she have?"

After a moment of studying Zach, Bernard took a puff on his cigar and blew the smoke out thoughtfully. The breeze immediately swept it away. "Well, no, I suppose not. I asked you here because the weekend before her death, I had hired her for a private party. She completely amazed my guests with some of the things she told them. I doubled her fee, I was so impressed. Very talented woman. When I came back in town and heard what happened, I was shocked. Such a loss. I wanted to extend my sympathies to you in person."

I watched Zach take him in, his guard still up. "Thank you. She will be missed."

Suddenly Bernard's face lit up as a tall, lithe woman with a silky black bob came toward us. Her eyes raked us over from behind a gold mask as she slipped her hand in the crook of Bernard's elbow.

"There you are, darling," Bernard said, patting her hand. "Remember the fortune teller from our last party, Rose Faraday? This is her son, Zach, and his date, Darwin Winters." His eyes glittered as he smiled at the woman. "This lovely creature is Nova Diaz."

Nova Diaz slipped her mask off to reveal flawless caramel skin and held out her hand to us. A gold band in the shape of a snake wrapped around her upper arm, two fairly large diamond eyes staring at me from the snake's head. Despite her beauty there was an edge to Ms. Diaz, an almost predatory intelligence that didn't usually come with arm candy.

"Nice to meet you." She spoke to Zach without a hint of a smile. "So sorry for your loss, Mr. Faraday. We were just stunned to hear of her passing."

I tried to read her emotions. There was no regret or empathy coming off of her. She didn't seem very sorry.

"I was telling Zach how impressed we all were with his mother's talent," Bernard continued. "She was an amazing woman."

"Yes. She was dead on with my reading," Nova said under her breath.

I glanced at Zach but he didn't appear to have heard her.

As Bernard Grayson talked on about Rose, I concentrated on Nova. Every now and then, I would feel something coming off of her, but she was obviously very practiced at keeping her guard up. Despite her cool outer appearance and flirty laughter, something darker occasionally slipped through her guard. Anger, maybe? Fear? I could never tell the difference between the two. They both felt like zillions of tiny pinpricks.

I mentally jumped back into the conversation when Bernard mentioned how they had met at a reptile convention in Tampa.

"Reptile convention?" Zach asked, also perking up.

Bernard nodded, puffing on his cigar. "I know it's hard to believe, considering what happened to your mother, but snakes really do make wonderful pets."

"And you have a pet snake?" I asked Nova.

"Yes, I actually have three at home now, two pythons and my newest gift from Bernard, a baby rainbow boa." She squeezed Bernard's arm affectionately. "Bernard has taught me so much about them. When we met I was just a curious novice. They really are like potato chips, you can't stop at one."

Bernard chuckled, his eyes sparkling. "Such passion, this one. And so true."

"How many do you have?" I asked Bernard.

"Well, let's see. Currently I have three green tree vipers and a Jararaca, which are all poisonous, and nineteen Brazilian rainbow boas which are not. Magnificent creatures. I'm a bit obsessed with them. They absolutely sparkle in the sunlight. I'm just a sucker for sparkle," he said, grinning and sliding his hand up Nova's arm.

"Do you buy them directly from Brazil?" I wanted to ask him if he had any rattlers, but that would have been too obvious.

He turned his eyes on me. "Yes, I do, actually. I like to see what I'm buying, not order something from a picture over the internet. I suppose that makes me eccentric."

Nova shot me a dark look then pulled Bernard's attention back to her. "And I'm a sucker for eccentric," she cooed.

What in heaven's name was that all about? I watched them together. They just didn't seem to fit. Nova wasn't on the list of people with a license to have dangerous reptiles either, but maybe she lived out of the area? Or felt like she was above the law.

"Darwin!" A familiar voice rang out from behind Bernard. He turned and I saw him extend his hand.

"Frankie, hello." It was good to see a familiar face. We hugged and I checked out her plum colored sequined gown. It clashed monumentally with her red hair, but somehow worked for her. "You look amazing. What are you doing here?"

"Oh, Jack and Bernard are golfing buddies. You remember Jack, right?"

"Of course, hi, Jack." I waved. *He sure did get around.* He and Bernard were laughing about something. Jack waved back and then squeezed Bernard's shoulder.

"Darwin." He sidled up next to Frankie and held out his hand to me. "Good to see you again. You look smashing!"

"Thank you." I shook his hand.

Frankie was staring curiously at Zach. "You're Zach Faraday, right? The psychic from Landon's Halloween bash?" Her eyes flicked to me, filling with questions.

"Yes. That's right." Zach downed the last of his martini.

"Oh, you're psychic, too?" Bernard showed a mouthful of bleached choppers. "I guess it runs in the family." His eyes moved to Nova. "How 'bout that, sweetheart?"

"Interesting," she said coolly.

Frankie moved closer to me and whispered, "What are you doing here with Zach, darlin'? Where's Will?"

"Long story," I whispered back. "Fill you in later."

By the time Mallory and I slid back into a cab it was after one in the morning. My exhausted brain felt like a rock in my skull, but I did know one thing. I had some new people to add to my suspect list.

CHAPTER EIGHTEEN

Saturday morning I called and scheduled an appointment with Lucky's vet since Zach had dug up her number for me. Turns out she was due for a rabies vaccine. Then I called Will. No answer. I knew he wasn't working, which meant he just didn't want to talk to me.

Sulking, I made a cup of tea and went outside to join Mallory and Lucky on the balcony. Mallory was strumming her guitar, lost in thought. Lucky was curled in a tight ball in the chair beside her.

"Morning, Mal." I slid Lucky over to join her on the chair. She meowed in protest. "Hey, kitty, it's my chair," I answered.

"Good morning." Mallory kept her eyes fixed on the park. "So, what do you think Zach Faraday's deal is? He's so creepy. And how does he know about Father?"

Seemed Zach Faraday had her hackles up, too. I stroked Lucky's side as she settled back down in my lap. It was the first time she had actually relaxed on me. I tried not to move and disturb her. "I don't know what to think about him, and I have no idea how he knows about Father. I definitely don't trust him, though."

Mallory rolled her head lazily to gaze at me. "He likes you, you know."

I frowned as I thought about what happened while we were dancing, the way he touched my face. "He might. But like I said, I don't trust him. There's something dark and secretive about him."

"And dangerous," Mallory added, strumming her guitar lightly.

"Yeah, and dangerous," I agreed. "Speaking of creepy, Bernard Grayson and his friends are really into snakes. Did you find out anything about the boa, Marsha?"

"Not much. Sammy said they've had her for about a month, and she eats the same thing as the other snakes. Frozen rats and mice. What kind of vision did you have?"

"It wasn't a vision this time. It was a really bad stomach pain."

"A snake with a stomachache?" Mallory's face scrunched up. "Maybe she ate a bad rat."

"I don't know if that's possible." I shrugged. "I guess I can ask the vet when I take Lucky in on Tuesday." I laid my head back and stared up at the baby blue sky full of wispy clouds. "It can't be a coincidence that Rose Faraday was at the Grayson house just a week before her death by snake bite. And Bernard Grayson is so into snakes. There has to be a connection there."

CHAPTER NINETEEN

Tuesday morning, I left Sylvia and Mallory to mind the pet boutique while Lucky and I took a cab to the Beachside Animal Clinic.

I checked us in and waited in the plastic chairs, reading all the posters on the walls about heartworms, ticks and other unseemly dangers to pets in Florida. Seems like everything in this state wanted to feed on you.

"Miss Winters?" A woman in Scooby Doo scrubs called to me. "We're ready to see Lucky."

She led us to a small room with a metal examination table and more scary posters. I hefted the carrier up onto the table and peered in at Lucky. "Don't be scared, you know this place, right?" She just stared at me suspiciously. At least her ears weren't back.

"Hello." The vet entered. She wore a white lab coat over her trim figure, her blonde hair swaying in a neat, chin-length bob. She held out a hand to me. "I'm Dr. Brown."

I shook her offered hand. "Darwin Winters. Nice to meet you."

"Hey there, Lucky." She unlatched the pet carrier door. "We wondered what happened to you." She pulled Lucky gently from the carrier and let her stretch on the table. "We heard about Rose and were just shocked. You never think such a thing can happen in the safety of your own home." A dark cloud passed over her face and she shook it off, stroking Lucky as the cat began to purr. "At least she's unharmed. So, did you adopt her, Darwin?"

"Well, she sort of adopted me and my sister. We found her the night Rose's body was discovered. She had apparently been frightened by the snake and escaped through a tear in the lanai screen."

Dr. Brown shook her head. "Good thing. Saved her own life."

"Yeah, but she does seem traumatized. She won't walk on the floor at all. She gets around the house by jumping on the furniture and counters. Do you think she'll ever recover?"

Dr. Brown watched Lucky thoughtfully. "Cats really don't like change and they do feel stress and separation anxiety. Losing her home and caretaker is a huge change. She may recover after having a stable environment again but it's hard to predict." She ran a hand over Lucky's back and tail. "Not shedding excessively. That's good. My suggestion would be just try to give her a stable routine, lots of affection and playtime. And just good old fashion time."

"No magic pill, huh?" I sighed.

"Afraid not." Dr. Brown gave me a consoling smile and then turned her attention back to Lucky. "Okay, little girl, let's get you caught up on your rabies shot." The vet tech came over to help hold

Lucky while Dr. Brown got the shot ready. "I think she's due for heartworm medication, also."

"Okay. Oh, also I wasn't sure what kind of food she's been on. Do you know? She seems to like tuna."

Dimples appeared when Dr. Brown smiled, which made her look too young to be a doctor. "Rose actually had her on lower calorie kibble mixed with some wet food. We sell it here. I'll have Carrie get that for you when you check out."

"Thanks." I busied myself looking at the photos on the wall above the counter as they gave Lucky her shot. Two little blonde girls in braids were smiling from each frame. "Precious little girls."

Dr. Brown scratched Lucky's head, while the vet tech whispered to her. "All done. What a good girl."

Dr. Brown glanced up at the photos I was referring to. "Thank you. Sidney's four and Sasha's six. They grow up so fast." She sighed, but a hint of a smile remained on her lips. "All right. We're all set here. I'm sure Rose would appreciate you taking such good care of Lucky. She really adored this cat." She helped coax Lucky back into the carrier. "I'd keep her indoors this time of year. Halloween is very unlucky for black cats. Do you have any other questions for me?"

"Oh, yes, actually I do, but it's not about Lucky. I was wondering, is it possible for a snake to get food poisoning?"

I had expected her to laugh or give me a strange look but she did neither. Instead, she became very still. "Why do you ask?"

Yes, why do I ask? "I, um, have a friend with a snake and he seems to think the snake is in pain, in the stomach. He's not eating. The snake, not my friend." I pressed my lips closed to keep from babbling anymore. Dr. Brown's demeanor had gone cold.

"Well, there are things that could be wrong," she said cautiously. "Constipation for one. Internal bacterial infections, parasites. The best thing to do is have your friend bring him in for a check-up."

"Okay, thank you. I appreciate the information." I was suddenly talking to her back as she exited the room. I shrugged. She must not be a big fan of snakes. I grabbed Lucky and carried her out to the counter to pay the bill and get her food and medication.

On the way out the door, I ran smack into Bernard's girlfriend as she was coming in.

I stuttered out an apology. "So sorry! Oh, Nova Diaz, right?"

She seemed taken aback. Her eyes widened a bit under a black ball cap. "Yes?"

"Darwin Winters. We met at Bernard's Masquerade Ball."

"Oh yes." Her gaze slid behind me and then down at the carrier. "The Masquerade Ball," she said, obviously distracted.

"This is Rose Faraday's cat, Lucky," I offered. "The fortune teller who was killed by the rattlesnake? She's sort of adopted me and my sister." Nova didn't say anything. She just stared at me. I could see something running through her mind as her expression darkened. I was holding the door open, and Lucky was growing heavier by the second. The silence was growing heavy, too. This was getting uncomfortable.

I cleared my throat. "Well, it was good to see you again." As I moved to push past her, she grabbed me. Her fingers dug into my arm.

"Miss Winters."

I lifted my gaze to hers, my heart suddenly hammering in my chest. "Yes?"

Her face was stone. "You and Zachary need to be careful. There are some things just better left alone."

Stunned, I just stood there like an idiot as I watched the door close behind her.

Did she just threaten me and Zach?

CHAPTER TWENTY

The next morning kept us pretty busy. The bells over the door were a steady background noise as customers came and went. At the table by the front window, the regulars sat with their dogs on their laps. I kept the table stocked with tea and snacks, for the humans and the pets. The buzz of conversation added to the hum of background noise in the boutique.

"Is getting *muita demente* in here, no?" Sylvia said with a grin, as she checked her next appointment time on the computer.

I laughed. "Very crazy, but in a good way." Mallory staggered over and plopped an armload of merchandise down on the counter. "This is for Mrs. Thornsbury." She raised an eyebrow. Her face was flushed and sweat darkened the hair around her face. "She's still shopping," she growled.

Sylvia chuckled and buttoned up the white coat she wore over a sleek flowered dress. "Okay. Just send Mr. Bojangles back when he gets here."

"Will do," I said. The door bells announced another customer. I glanced up in time see a generous bouquet of flowers moving through the door. When they got to the counter, a face appeared behind them.

"Looking for Miss Winters," the delivery man said.

"Oh, that's me."

"Perfect." He sat the glass vase down on the last empty counter space. The flowers' sweet scent filled my nose. "Enjoy."

"Thank you." I pressed my nose into an orange lily. *Mmmmm. Who sent these?* I plucked the card out and read: *We should talk. Thinking of you, Will.*

My heart soared, and I couldn't stop myself from grinning like a school girl. Yes, we should talk, definitely. I had stopped leaving messages after about the twentieth one went unreturned. But, now he wanted to talk. And he was thinking of me. Did the sun just come out? In my life, it had.

I scooped the vase off the front counter and moved it behind me where it wouldn't get knocked over. Mallory returned with another armful of stuff. She glanced from the flowers to me.

"From the mile-wide grin on your face, I take it those are from Will."

"Yes," I almost squealed. I tried to compose myself and keep from floating up to the ceiling. "He wants us to talk."

"Wonderful," she answered, smirking. "Well, since you're in such a good mood, this would be a good time to tell you that Sammy asked me out. We're going to dinner Friday night." She scooted away before I could object.

Well, that would be something we would discuss tonight. There was no way my little sister was going on a date with an older man. At least, not without me chaperoning. I was looking in the direction of the door as a short, dark haired lady walked in carrying a Lhasa Apso puppy in her arms. She looked familiar but I didn't recognize her puppy. *Where did I know her from?*

She glanced over the store and then made her way down the far left wall. Mrs. Thornsbury came to the counter, her gray bun coming undone, her silvery eyes sparkling within a wrinkled face. "I think I'm all set, dear."

"Great." I smiled and started to ring up her purchases. "You didn't bring Happy in with you today?"

"No, poor thing got into a red ant nest in the yard and got all bit up. He had an allergic reaction to the bites, bless his heart. He's home recovering after spending the night at the vets."

"Oh, no, that's just awful." I glanced over the store as I bagged her purchases. "Hey, Mal?"

Mallory peered out from behind an aisle. "Yeah?"

"Can you grab me a bottle of Recovery?"

She had the flower essence in my hand in a flash. She really was working hard. I felt a stab of gratefulness that she was here.

"Thanks," I said. "Okay, I'm going to give you a bottle of this flower essence at no charge. You can rub a few drops in Happy's skin every few hours and also mix some with water in a squirt bottle and spritz his bedding and surrounding area. It will help keep his anxiety and stress down as he recovers." I wrapped it in tissue and placed it in her bulging bag.

"Oh, thank you, Darwin." Her gray eyes watered. "He's all the family I've got left. Thank you for being such a dear."

"That's what we're here for, Mrs. Thornsbury." I smiled at her as she patted my hand. "You take care of that boy and bring him in to see us when he's feeling better."

"Oh, you know I will, he's gonna need a good grooming," she said. "See you girls soon."

The dark haired lady was next in line. "Hi," I greeted her and tried to place her. "Did you find everything okay?"

"Yes," she answered, dropping a pink harness and leash on the counter. "My daughter, she thinks I need company." She mumbled under her breath. "Gave me dis puppy." She smiled down at the ball of gray and white fur panting and wiggling in her arms. "I say I have enough responsibilities but she doesn't listen. What can you do?"

Ah, I got it. The accent. "She sure is a cutie." I reached over the counter and scratched her little furry head. "Hey, don't you work for Mr. Bernard Grayson?"

"Yes," she answered, eyeing me. "Ah, you were at the Masquerade Ball, yes?"

"I was." I held out my hand. "Darwin. Nice to see you again." We shook and I lifted up the harness. "Here, let me cut the tags off these so you don't have to carry her around. What did you name her?"

"Thank you. Her name is Bianca." She dug through her purse and pulled out a well-worn leather wallet. "Mr. Bernard, he loves to throw parties."

"Do you live in the house?"

"No. I stay in the guest house in the back."

"Well, just make sure you keep that little girl away from all the snakes." I shuddered involuntarily. "You don't have to take care of them, too, do you?"

"No no." She shook her head. "No one is allowed in their housing area except for Mr. Bernard." She handed me her debit card. "Not even his new girlfriend. I heard them fighting one night after a big party. He was very upset with Miss Diaz because after the party she went into the snake house. Big fight." She shrugged her shoulders. "He must be in love because she is still around."

I smiled as I handed her a receipt and grooming coupon. "He did look smitten with her at the Ball. Does she live there?" My mind was reeling as she slid the new harness on Bianca and clipped on the lead.

"No. She live at Beachgate condos. Ah, much better!" She chuckled as the puppy lapped around her in circles. She turned around to keep from getting tangled in the new leash. "Or maybe not." She picked Bianca back up. "We'll work on it. Thank you for your help."

"You're welcome." I had one more question for her. "Wait, just one more thing. That party you mentioned, when Bernard and his girlfriend got it the fight, was there a fortune teller there that night?"

She nodded thoughtfully. "Yes, there was. She had the house buzzing like a beehive. Mr. Bernard and his friends, they say she told them things no one should know." She lowered her voice. "Me? I think she talks with the devil."

I nodded. "Thank you. Enjoy your new baby, and we'll see you soon."

Interesting. So, Nova snuck into Bernard's snake house after the party Rose entertained at? Could Nova have been trying to steal a poisonous snake then? Why didn't Bernard allow anyone in the snake house? Not even his girlfriend? I guess he could just be worried about someone getting hurt. But, why did it feel more sinister than that?

CHAPTER TWENTY-ONE

All week I tried to piece together the clues I had gathered so far. Well, all week in between dealing with the mad house Darwin's Pet Boutique, and Beach Drive in general, had become. Tourist season was in full swing and it was rocking our world. By the time we turned the closed sign around on the door every evening, we were all exhausted and the boutique looked like a tornado had gone through, flinging stuff everywhere.

The treat table had two lonely boxes left, the tiny shirts and waterproof jackets were draped over hangers or lying on the floor beneath them, boxes had stacked up that we hadn't had time to open yet. Oy. My feet were aching and my cheeks hurt from smiling.

"Tea?" I asked Sylvia as I slumped down at the table in front of the window and kicked off my leather wedge sandals. I had decided shoes were evil.

Sylvia peeled off her white coat and let out a string of Portuguese on a sigh. "I'm going home to a hot bath and bottle of wine. What are you up to tonight?"

Mallory yelled from somewhere in the store. "I have a date!" Then she came around the aisle just in time to catch me rolling my eyes.

"A date?" Sylvia raised a dark eyebrow at her.

"Yep. With a handsome, rich guy with amazing eyes who is crazy about me." She stuck her tongue out at me and I narrowed my eyes at her.

"I'm chaperoning this date." I stirred my tea with more vigor. I was hoping Will would have called me this week and we could have made it a double date. But, he didn't so it wasn't.

"Who is this guy?" Sylvia perched one hand on a curvy hip.

"His name is Sammy Harris and he's a perfect gentleman," Mallory answered.

"He better be," I mumbled. I wasn't worried about Mallory's physical safety. She could more than take care of herself in that department. It was her heart I was worried about. She was such a passionate person, so vulnerable to jumping in head first and getting her heart broken. *Yeah, like I was one to talk.*

"Ay yi yi," Sylvia sighed. "There is no such thing as a perfect gentleman, my *menina amiga*." She folded up her white coat. "Where is this date going to happen?"

"At Parkshore Grill and then back home," I said pointedly to Mallory. "To our home, not his."

Mallory glared at me. "Will you relax, please? You sound like Mom. Of course, I wouldn't go to his house on a first date. Can you give me some credit?"

"You are lucky to have a sister who worries about you." Sylvia put an arm around Mallory and kissed the top of her head. "You be safe." She grabbed her purse and keys from under the counter. "I'll see you *amigas* tomorrow."

I sighed and put my tea down. "All right, let us go get ready for your date."

* * *

Temperatures had dropped as night fell so Mallory and I opted for a table inside the warmth of Parkshore Grill. We weren't seated long before Sammy rolled through the door, looking like he just stepped out of GQ magazine in dark slacks and a buttery suede blazer. Mallory's face flushed and her eyes brightened. *Oh good grief. Is that how I looked around Will?*

"Good evening, ladies." Sammy smiled as he took a seat next to Mallory, lifted her hand and kissed it. My hackles raised and my eyes narrowed. He completely ignored my reaction, and instead he glanced at the empty seat next to me. The waiter came over and asked what we would like to drink. "Should we get something for your date?"

Was he trying to be funny? I wasn't amused.

"Oh," Mallory jumped in. "Will just called. He can't make it. Got called in to work." She looked at me sheepishly, and I realized that Mallory had told Sammy this would be a double date, not her big sister chaperoning.

I ordered a glass of wine. This was going to be a long night.

"So, Sammy." I folded my arms and rested my elbows on the table. "What do you do when you're not at the Serpentarium?"

"Well," he answered, looking at Mallory, not me. "I fish. You should come out on my boat next weekend. I'm sure you'd love it." He turned to me as the waiter brought our drinks. "You, too, Darwin. There's nothing like spending a day in the open ocean."

He was right about that. I imagined a big wave rising up and swallowing him and his boat. I shook it off. *Stop it, Darwin.* Why did I dislike this guy so much? Was it just because I was feeling protective of Mallory? He'd never given me another reason to dislike him. Mallory was right. I was being judgmental.

"Sounds fun," I said. I decided I needed to just get to know him better. "So, what do you do for work?"

"I'm a pilot. I fly Bernard Grayson's private plane. Doesn't feel like work, really. Feels more like I get paid to go on mini-vacations." He smiled at Mallory. "Not a very dignified job, I know." He took a sip of the rum and coke he had ordered.

"Dignified is overrated." Mallory smiled back.

"So," I said casually, "Mr. Grayson had mentioned that he was shocked to come back to St. Pete and hear the news about Rose Faraday being killed by a rattlesnake. Did you fly him somewhere at that time?"

Sammy gave me a strange look. "Oh, yeah. We had just got back from Brazil. Bernard's gotten obsessed with the Brazilian rainbow boa." He nodded. "Yeah, you hate to hear about a freak accident like that. Makes people fear snakes and they're more likely to kill them instead of just leave them alone." He frowned. "Oh, speaking of snakes. You were asking my partner, McGillis, if it was possible the rattler that bit Rose Faraday could have escaped from someone?"

I nodded and tried not to seem too eager for the information. "Yes?"

"Well, I talked to Jet Jamison and he did have one get away from him, a rattler. Though don't tell him I told you that. He could get fined if someone found out. He caught two of them himself and hadn't had time to microchip them before one escaped. So, if it was his, I guess that would explain why there was a rattler in a populated area."

"Yeah, I guess that would explain it." But it didn't explain why someone slipped the snake into Rose's lanai in the middle of the night. Was that someone Jet Jamison? If so, what was his connection to Rose? Or did someone hire him to do it? "So, are you going to give Jet Jamison back the rattler?"

"No. He said to keep her, she's bad juju now that she's killed somebody." He chuckled. "If you believe in that sort of thing."

"Some people are so superstitious." Mallory rolled her eyes.

Grabbing a menu off the table, he changed the subject. "I don't know about you girls, but I'm starving. A nice fat filet mignon sounds good."

"Sounds good to me, too," Mallory said. She made eye contact with me and mouthed the word "pilot," practically swooning.

I raised my brow at her, though I did crack a smile. She seemed so happy. And if Sammy and Bernard Grayson were out of town the night Rose died, I could cross them off my suspect list and not worry so much about Mallory dating Sammy. I'd have to verify it for sure somehow. But for now, I ordered a Caesar salad and decided to stay in the background as much as possible.

"So you live in Savannah?" Sammy's full attention was back on Mallory.

"Yep."

"How long will you be in St. Pete?"

"Oh, I don't know. I'm not in any hurry to get back. I like it here."

I played with my phone as they chatted and got to know each other better. I was shocked really, at how open Mallory was being with him. I mean, she didn't tell him who our father was, but she did tell him that he left us. That we grew up fatherless. I hadn't even told Will that yet. I heard their conversation wind back to his investment in the Serpentarium. Apparently, he'd always been interested in snakes so he'd decided to help his buddy out financially with the place.

Our food came. We ate, they talked some more and laughed. I was sipping my wine, and rethinking the whole idea of hiding who I was from Will, when Sammy's phone buzzed on the table.

He glanced at it. I could see the struggle on his face and finally he sighed. "I'm sorry, Mallory, I have to get this." He picked up the phone. "Yeah."

Mallory had her chin resting on her fist as she grinned at me. I smiled back. It was nice to see her practically glowing.

"What?" It was more like a gasp than a word. We both looked at Sammy. His normally tanned face had paled. He rose slowly from the table and stumbled to the back of the restaurant.

Mallory and I shared a concerned look.

"I wonder what that was all about?" she whispered.

I bit my lip. "The restrooms are back there. I'll be right back."

"No—"

I slid out of the chair and made my way to the back before she could protest. For all she knew I really did have to use the ladies' room, I reasoned. As I came around the corner I saw Sammy slam the men's room door open with a loud expletive. I slipped into the door marked "women" and pressed my ear to the wall between the two restrooms hoping I could hear something. An elderly woman entered and gave me a strange look before disappearing into a stall. I sighed, defeated. I couldn't hear a thing.

After waiting the proper amount of time, I returned to the table and found Mallory there alone, her face all scrunched up in worry.

"Where's Sammy?"

"He had to go. There was an emergency, apparently. He looked really upset. Said he would call me when he could."

"He didn't tell you what happened?"

"No."

"Oh, well then." I rummaged through my straw bag. "I'll just take care of the bill and we can get out of here."

"He already paid it," Mallory said, still looking dejected.

I put a hand over hers. "I'm sure everything will be fine. I'm sure he'll call you when he can. He does seem like a nice guy, Mal."

She rewarded my concession with a smile and squeeze of my hand. "He does, doesn't he? All right. Let's get out of here."

CHAPTER TWENTY-TWO

Saturday evening, I called Frankie to come pick me up to do a little sleuthing. Her toy-like red sports car purred out front within a half hour. I knew she couldn't resist an adventure.

"Not sure we're going to be very inconspicuous in this moving firecracker," I teased her as I slid into the soft leather seat.

She chuckled. "I could have brought the limo."

"Guess we'll have to take our chances." I shook my head as Frankie maneuvered the little convertible out into the heavy Beach Drive traffic.

"Speakin' of firecrackers, what's that little sister of yours up to tonight?"

"I left her minding the oven and playing fetch with Lucky on the sofa."

"Lucky the cat? She plays fetch?"

"Yeah. With Mallory's hair ties. She is a funny little creature. Lots of personality. Really traumatized by this whole mess, though."

"Animals understand more than we give 'em credit for, that's for sure," Frankie said. "Mallory okay with you leaving her out of tonight's fun?"

"Yeah, she didn't mind. She's exhausted and we've got a whole lot of treats to bake this weekend. The boutique has been a mad house."

Plus, she was still pouting about Sammy not calling her, but I didn't mention that.

"Glad to hear it." Frankie punched the horn as a large silver car drifted into her lane. They waved. Guess they hadn't seen her. Maybe we could be inconspicuous after all. "I mean, glad to hear business is good. Wouldn't want you gals going anywhere. Oh, speaking of... where exactly are we going and what are we doing?"

"Oh, yeah. Do you know where the Beachgate condos are?"

"Sure."

"Okay, we're going there to see if we can find out where Nova Diaz lives and spy on her."

Frankie was silent for a moment. "Nova Diaz? Bernard's girlfriend? Whatever for?"

I watched the moonlight drift on the bay waters. "Do you know her?"

"Well, I've met her a few times at Bernard's house. She's always been polite. Bernard is definitely head over heels for her. Jack says he's never seen the guy so happy before. What's up?"

How much could I tell her? It was getting exhausting hiding things from my friends. "Well, the reason I was at Bernard's Masquerade Ball with Zach Faraday was because Zach believes his mother was murdered. That someone let that rattlesnake into her condo on purpose."

"What?" She turned to me, her eyes wide. "Seriously? Why would he think that?"

"Well, you know he is psychic." I knew she believed that. I let it speak for itself.

"True." She took in a deep breath. "So, what does that have to do with Nova?"

"We found out that Rose Faraday had been hired to be the entertainment at Bernard's house the weekend before her death. Seems like a big coincidence that she was killed by a snake the weekend after being at the home of a man who owns so many snakes, and has a bunch of friends with snakes, doesn't it?"

"Yeah, I guess it does seem like an odd coincidence."

"So, Bernard's housekeeper told me the night Rose was the entertainment at Bernard's house, Nova snuck into the snake house. Apparently she and Bernard got in a big fight because he doesn't allow anyone in the snake house."

"So, you're thinking she snuck the rattler from there?"

"That's what I need to find out."

"But why would she do that?"

"I don't know. Maybe Rose saw something that night she wasn't supposed to. Or maybe she made Nova mad? Hard to figure out what goes on in the mind of a killer. Besides, Nova really seems like she's hiding something. Oh, and Nova did make a comment at the Ball that Rose was dead on with her reading. She didn't sound very happy about it either. Like maybe Rose knew what she was hiding. And," I turned in the compact seat to face Frankie, "I ran into her at Lucky's vet's office and she threatened me and Zach to leave things alone."

Frankie's makeup creased around her eyes as she frowned and turned into the entrance to

Beachgate condos. "She always seemed so nice. That doesn't sound like her. Why would she say that?" Frankie made a left into the wide, flat parking area. "Do we know which condo is hers?"

"No." I sighed. "I was hoping we could stake out the parking lot and catch her coming home."

Frankie held up a freckled hand, a large gold and diamond bracelet sliding down her arm. "Just so happens I can help with that. I've seen her drive a white BMW, so we know what kind of car to watch for."

I grinned. "I knew there was a reason I called you."

Frankie backed into a space where we had a good view of the palm tree lined entrance. "Also," she turned off the engine and pulled an insulated beach tote from behind my seat, "I brought snacks."

I laughed. "Of course you did." I was surprised she didn't have Itty and Bitty back there as well.

We sat there under the stars, enjoying the night air, catching up on each other's lives and munching on brie, grapes and sesame crackers.

"So you really like Jack?" I asked.

"Sure. He's fun to hang out with. He's not looking for a relationship, though. He's a bit of a player which is fine by me. I'm enjoying just worrying about me and my girls. No crazy man drama to deal with."

I couldn't blame her after the way her last relationship turned out. We perked up as car lights turned in. Nope. Not the white BMW.

I took a sip from a mini-water bottle. "Has Jack ever mentioned to you how much he disliked Rose Faraday?"

She turned to me, swallowing and shaking her head. "No. Not until his conversation with you at Landon's Halloween party. Something about her making dog owner's lives miserable at their condos?"

"Yeah. Apparently Rose was president of the HOA there. She implemented this program where all the dogs had to have their DNA on file and if any doggie mess was found, it would be tested and the culprit would be fined $1,000. If they didn't pay, their dog could be confiscated."

"Oh, that's what he was talking about?" Frankie looked like she didn't know whether to laugh or be angry. "That's ridiculous."

"That's not the worst part. Apparently, Rose threatened to poison Jack's dog, Monkey."

Frankie's face turned red. Now she was angry. "Well, if she went around threatening to poison people's pets, it wouldn't surprise me if someone offed her." She bit into a cracker violently. Tiny bits of it sprayed the dashboard. "I just don't understand some people."

"Me either, Frankie." I sighed and repositioned my legs. My hip had gone to sleep and was tingling. *Where in heavens was Nova tonight? What if she was spending the night at Bernard's place?*

Frankie squinted as another car entered the lot and parked. White but not a BMW. "Well, Jack's the president now so the residents don't have to worry about her threatening their pets anymore."

Yeah. That's what worried me. That was a pretty solid motive for murder in my book.

* * *

Around midnight we were tired of sitting, and getting ready to throw in the towel, when the white BMW pulled into the parking lot.

"Get down!" Frankie clutched my arm and we ducked as the car lights swooped over us. The car slid into a space two spots down from us. We listened for the door to shut and then raised our heads up.

"It's her," I whispered. "Let's go."

We jumped out and ducked behind her car. Frankie peered over the hood. "Okay, she's at the walkway. Come on."

We made a wide arch through the parking lot so we could get a better view of which condo she entered. She paused at a door, keys in her hand.

"I think this is it," I whispered. Nova turned suddenly and looked our way. Frankie pulled me down behind a truck. We were breathing heavy and I felt ridiculous. If someone saw us, they would probably call the police. "Do you think she spotted us?"

"Don't know." Frankie got down on her hands and knees and crawled out from behind the tire. I bit my lip and tried not to giggle at the sight of her leopard print derriere sticking up in the air. "She's going in."

We rushed forward just as the door to condo number fourteen was closing. I held up my hand for a high five.

Frankie smacked it with a huge grin. "Bingo!" Then we both stared at the door, our hands on our hips, our breathing shallow. "Now what?"

Time to spy. "Let's go around back, see if there's a window to peek in."

As we silently made our way around the back of the building, trying to stay hidden and counting the condos to find number fourteen, Frankie nudged me. "I hope you have Will's number on speed dial if we get caught."

"Not sure he'd pick up the phone," I mumbled, stepping over a prickly pear cactus. "We kind of had a fight about Zach."

"He's not jealous of Zach, is he?"

I shrugged and swatted at a mosquito buzzing around my face. "I don't know. I think it's more like he doesn't like me keeping things from him. I should have told him sooner that we believed Rose had been murdered."

"Well, he does seem like the kind of guy that appreciates full disclosure. That's an easy thing to fix, though. Just tell him everything. I'm sure you two will be back canoodling in no time."

Yeah, easy for someone without crazy secrets to say. I glanced at Frankie as we arrived at the back of the condo. "Canoodling?"

She grinned and pointed at the sliding glass door then gave me a thumbs up. The blinds were slanted open enough that shards of yellow light spilled out onto the patio. We snuck up to the patio and plastered ourselves against the peach stucco wall on either side of the sliding doors. I nodded and we both peeked in.

Through the slats in the blinds, I spotted Nova sitting on the sofa in a flowery yellow dress. She was busy with something on the coffee table in front of her, but I couldn't see past the edge of an overstuffed chair to see what it was. I scanned the room behind her. Two large aquariums sat against the wall, lights hung over them. Must be her snakes. I mentally kicked myself for not bringing binoculars. I would have loved to see what kind of snakes were actually in there. I glanced over at Frankie. She was motioning furiously at me.

"What?" I mouthed. I decided she probably had a better view so I scurried around the patio furniture and glued myself to the wall next to her. "What is it?"

Frankie pulled me in front of her. I peered through the blinds at the new angle and my heart leapfrogged into my throat. Now I could see what she was doing. She was expertly cleaning a gun.

CHAPTER TWENTY-THREE

Yawning, I ran a feather duster over the pet boutique countertops, computer monitor and counter items: jars of impulse treats, a basket of hand-crafted Halloween-shaped cat toys, bumper stickers for pet lovers and a myriad of other things for sale. I wasn't sure how long I had been dusting, lost in thought, until a knock on the door startled me. A quick glance at the time told me we still had twenty minutes before opening. I mumbled to myself as I walked around to see who was there.

Zach threw up a quick wave. *Heavens, what was he doing here?* I motioned for him to give me a second and went to retrieve the keys.

"You're out and about early." I frowned as I let him in. "Everything all right? Want some tea?" I helped myself to a cup, motioning for him to have a seat in a chair in front of the window.

He settled into the chair. "No tea, thank you." He wore a fitted gray t-shirt, black jeans and cowboy boots. It suited him.

"So, what's up?"

One brow raised as his eyes raked over my body. "Your shirt is on inside out."

I glanced down and felt my face heat up. Yep, there were the seams and backsides of three buttons. I blinked and forced a laugh. "Guess I shouldn't get dressed in the dark."

His head tilted and a genuine look of concern narrowed his eyes. "Having trouble sleeping?"

"No, no." I waved off his concern, though I knew the shadows under my eyes betrayed me. The curse of pale skin. "I'm fine. So, what brings you here?"

Zach relaxed back into the chair and folded his hands in his lap with a little shrug. "Just want to compare notes. Find out any new information this weekend?"

"Yes. You?"

"Yes."

I blinked at him over my tea cup. I still didn't trust him. "Well?"

He seemed amused suddenly. "I followed Bernard Grayson and his woman friend to Albert Whitted Airport yesterday morning. I couldn't get through the gate, but my contact there told me they were headed to Brazil."

"Well, nothing surprising about that. That's where he buys his snakes." But, seriously, how many snakes did one man need? "Was Sammy Harris the pilot?"

"That I don't know," Zach answered. "But most likely."

I bit the inside of my cheek, thinking. "We had dinner with Sammy Friday night. He's sort of dating my sister. He got an emergency call and had to leave. So maybe someone else flew them. Mallory hasn't heard from him yet."

"Anything is possible." Zach let his gaze wander to the window and then back to me. "Did you find something out at this dinner?"

I sipped my tea and nodded. "Sammy mentioned the rattler that killed your mother probably came from a man named Jet Jamison. Apparently he captures them in the wild. His story was one got loose after he brought it back to St. Pete. That would explain why it was so close to civilization but not microchipped." I shook my head. "But still doesn't explain why Jamison said it got loose when someone actually slipped it into her lanai in the middle of the night."

I realized my mistake too late. My face flushed.

Zach's attention shifted back to me with laser precision. His eyes darkened. "It's time for full disclosure, Darwin. What do you know about that night that you aren't telling me?"

I was about to deny knowing anything more when I realized that the idea of actually being honest with someone about my gift was very appealing. And Zach already knew more than anyone else about me, besides my family. He seemed to know about my father. Plus his mother was a psychic. If there was ever anyone I could confide it, it was probably him.

I sat my cup down and looked him square in the eyes. "Okay." Deep breath. "When we found Lucky that night and I touched her..." I repositioned myself in the chair and tucked a short wave of hair behind my ear. *What's the simplest way to explain this?* "Well, if an animal has experienced recent trauma and I touch them, I get visions of whatever it is that hurt them or scared them. Pictures, feelings or sometimes smells. So when I touched Lucky, I saw a person in a dark hooded jacket putting the rattler on the lanai through a cut in the screen. Lucky apparently ran through that same hole to escape the snake. That's how she got out." I pressed my lips together and waited for him to respond.

Zach stared at me for a long moment. "And you have not shared this with your homicide detective boyfriend?"

I blinked, squirming under the heap of guilt that question buried me in. "No, I have not."

His mouth twitched, but it wasn't a smirk. "You don't think he would believe you?"

I sighed, suddenly tired. "Either way, it wouldn't work out in my favor. He would either not believe me and think I was a crazy person, or he would believe me and know I was a crazy person. I know it's a selfish reason." I glanced up at him. "But, you believe me?"

"Of course," he said. "You are part Elemental." The casual way he said this lifted something off my heart. It was so nice hearing someone, outside of my family, believe me and accept who I was. All of me. The human part and the secret part.

Tears sprang to my eyes. I blinked them back. *Get a grip, Darwin.* "Thank you," I whispered. "And I'm sorry for not telling Will. If I had, he might be looking for your mother's killer right now."

"If he actually believed you. Which is unlikely." Zach leaned forward and rested a hand on mine. It felt like a heat lamp had just switched on. I should have pulled away, but frankly it felt comforting. "We will find some hard evidence to take to him. No need for him to think of you as a crazy person."

I fought the urge to hug him and then I remembered last night. "Oh, also Frankie and I staked out Nova Diaz's place last night. That woman definitely isn't who she appears to be. She was sitting on her sofa messing with a gun. And she looked like she knew what she was doing." I didn't mention her warning to me and him. I figured the gun thing was enough. Why make him worry more?

Zach's brows raised and then he frowned. "You put yourself in danger." He leaned back in the chair. "Can I ask why you care to help find my mother's killer? You didn't even know her."

I blinked, not expecting that question. "Why? Because I'm the only one who knows it wasn't a freak accident. I couldn't live with myself if I just let it go, let someone get away with murder."

Zach shook his head and rubbed his hands on his jeans. "Okay. I'm staying in my mother's condo." He stood up, fished a card out of his wallet and dropped it on the table. "Well, I guess it's my condo now. If you find out anything else, you can contact me there or call me." He slipped his hand in mine and pulled me up to stand with him. "Or if you just want some company." His eyes held mine. Too close. I couldn't take in a full breath. I felt like a rabbit, frozen, trying to stay invisible to the fox. I managed a nod. Mercifully he backed away. "I'll let myself out."

I watched him out the window as he disappeared down the sidewalk. My insides were swirling with a mixture of relief he was gone, guilt for confiding in him and a strange feeling of happiness that he knew who I was and didn't judge me. I shook it off and flipped the Open sign over.

CHAPTER TWENTY-FOUR

Wednesday was All Hallows Eve. This was the first year I was actually enjoying Halloween and not dreading the tomatoes that would be thrown at our house in Savannah, or all the kids who would dare each other to ring our doorbell and, when we'd open the door to give them candy, run screaming back through the yard. Mallory had always spent Halloween crying in her room, though she would never admit it. Willow didn't seem to care one way or the other.

Halloween in St. Pete was fun. People were in good spirits, already walking around in costumes, toting around kids with painted faces during the day. We gave a treat to every pet that came in and had a bucket of candy for the humans, too.

I was in good spirits, too. Will had called me last night and apologized for not calling sooner. He was wrapping up a case and would be free tonight. We were going to have dinner and talk. I wasn't sure what I was going to say to him, but I was leaning more and more toward the truth. At least about how I knew Rose was murdered. The thought of that conversation made my palms sweat.

Mallory brought an armful of organic cat food to the counter, a small man trailing behind her. "Mr. Boseman needs something to stop Elizabeth Taylor from pulling hair out of her tail."

"Oh, poor kitty." I winked at Mallory. "The cherry plum and chicory mix should help."

"Be right back." She patted Mr. Boseman on the arm. "Darwin will ring you up."

I eyed the elderly man thoughtfully. "Have you moved or changed anything in Elizabeth Taylor's environment that would cause her stress, Mr. Boseman?"

His watery Basset Hound eyes blinked at me. "My son helped me move my living room furniture around a few weeks back. That's about all that's changed for us in ten years."

I smiled. "Well, that could be enough to cause her to over-groom from anxiety, but you might want to have your vet check her over just to be sure y'all aren't dealing with a skin disease."

"Here we are." Mallory handed me the brown bottle to wrap up, plucked a tootsie pop from the bowl of candy on the counter and handed it to him. "And Happy Halloween!"

I watched her bop over to another customer and smiled to myself. She was on cloud nine. Sammy had finally called her last night. They were going out tonight. She promised she would stay in a public place and begged me to let them go out alone. I caved. Truth be told, I wanted to spend time alone with Will, too. I did make her promise to text me every hour and let me know she was safe and to be home by 11:00. She had rolled her eyes but agreed.

After we closed up the pet boutique, we raced upstairs to the townhouse to shower and change. I had settled on a peach sundress and slipped into it as Lucky moved from my pillow to curl up on the pile of rejected clothes on the bed.

I clipped my white-blonde bangs back with a gold barrette and swooped my eyelashes with some mascara. "Don't get comfy on there, Lucky." I threw on a cream sweater over the dress and scratched her behind the ear. She squinted at me and stretched out on the pile. "Fine, stay there. Gives me a good excuse not to hang them back up right now." I grabbed a pair of gold hoop earrings off the dresser and padded down the stairs for my bag and flip-flops.

"You look very pretty, Mal." I said, meeting her in the kitchen. "Where are you two off to?"

"You, too." She smiled and hugged me. "Dinner and then movie. They're playing Halloween in Straub Park on a giant screen at 10:00. Thanks for not chaperoning, by the way." She smoothed my hair behind my ear like mom used to do. "Come clean with him, Sis."

I sighed. "When did you get so grown up?"

A smile lit up her face. I scooted her out of the kitchen. "Have fun. Be safe. Don't forget to text me."

I checked the clock after she left. Half an hour until I met Will. The townhouse felt suddenly too quiet and my own self-doubt was beginning to talk. Time to skedaddle.

CHAPTER TWENTY-FIVE

The walkways and streets were packed. The air held just a hint of a chill. The sky was a clear, wide open canvas for all the stars. I took in a deep breath as I made my way through the crowds next door to the Parkshore Grill. It would be a great night to sit outside and people watch. As I neared their outdoor tables with the blue umbrellas, my heart skipped. Will must have had the same idea. He had arrived early and was already seated outside, waiting for me.

"Hi." The word got stuck in my throat as I greeted him. He stood and stared down at me, drinking in my face like he hadn't seen me for a year. I bit my bottom lip. No one had ever looked at me like that before. His blue eyes swelled with emotion. I suddenly felt so guilty for causing him pain. I wanted to blurt out everything. I didn't want my secrets to be the wall between us anymore. I had to fix this.

"Hi," he whispered, trying to smile. It didn't reach his eyes.

"Will, I'm so sorry—" His mouth on mine halted the words. His lips were warm and gentle. I slipped my arms around his waist as he deepened the kiss. The muscles in his back were hard and tense beneath a cotton polo shirt. When he finally pulled away and rested his forehead on mine, my legs were trembling.

"God I've missed you." He cleared the emotion from his throat, slipped his hand in mine and motioned to the chair.

We sat down, but still held hands, neither one of us willing to let go. That is, until two waiters arrived, one with a bottle of wine and one with a tray of steaming, mouth watering appetizers.

Our hands slid apart to make room for the food.

"Thank you," Will said to the waiters as they arranged the offerings on the table. To me he said, "I got here a bit early so I ordered us something to start with. Hope you don't mind."

"Not at all." My stomach rumbled. "Mmm, is that goat cheese spinach dip?" I unrolled my napkin and found my weapon of choice. A fork. "And blue crab cake? Oh, yum." I slid a crab cake onto my plate and dug into it. "You do know how to get to a girl's heart, Detective Blake. Delicious."

"And a nice Ca Bolani Pinot." The lanky waiter smiled down at us as he uncorked the bottle. "I'll be back in a bit to take your dinner orders. Enjoy."

Will lifted his glass and invited me with his eyes to do the same. I swallowed and lifted my glass. "To new beginnings."

We clinked glasses. "New beginnings," I repeated. We locked eyes over our wine glasses. When we put them down, Will sighed.

"Look, Darwin. I've been doing a lot of soul searching lately. I know that my failed marriage and my ex-wife leaving me the way she did has caused issues for me. Trust issues, for one. But it's not fair of me to shut down and push you away just because you don't fully disclose everything in your life to me." I tried to butt in but he held up his hand. "Let me get this out. I'll admit, I was jealous when you told me you were going out with Mr. Faraday and that was a new emotion for me." He shook his head like he was still trying to wrap his mind around it. "And then when you told me about your little conspiracy theory that you two shared about his mother actually being murdered... well, that just pushed me over the edge."

I stiffened at his use of the words "conspiracy theory" but I kept silent and let him go on.

"I realized that you'll share things with me as you feel closer to me and trust me. That's the way this thing works, right? And I just have to be patient and not so quick to think you're keeping things from me on purpose. And we never agreed not to date other people, so I had no right getting upset."

Oh, heaven on a cracker. The cogs on my guilt wheels were really churning now. I squirmed and offered him a small smile.

He seemed to sense my discomfort and reached across to take my hand. His touch sent tiny vibrations through me that filled me with peace, like when two waves are in sync and hum together at perfect pitch. I felt my body relax as I lost myself in his eyes. Being with him, here in this moment, made me feel like I do when I'm immersed in water. Completely at home. In my element.

"But..." He pulled his hand away.

I started to panic. *But? No, no buts!*

"I don't have much room in my life for anything but work, and I've liked it that way. Until now." He slipped a tiny black velvet box out from its hiding place under his napkin. "Because of you. And I don't want to share you with anyone." He popped open the box. Nestled in the silk lining sat a silver ring with a small, square dark purple amethyst. It was gorgeous. "I know it might seem kind of high-schoolish, but this is a promise ring. I want to give it to you as a reminder of this promise. I promise to keep my heart open and be patient." He removed the ring and sat the box on the table. "And make our relationship exclusive." His smile was warm and soft as he shook his head and rubbed my ring finger. "This ring reminded me of your eyes. What do you say?"

I returned his warm smile, blinking back the tears. It didn't seem high-schoolish to me at all. I'd never gotten a promise ring before. We were home schooled but still, I'd never gotten any kind of present from a guy before. "Oh, Will, I don't need a ring to make our relationship exclusive. I've never met anyone like you and don't want to date anyone else." I glanced down at his promise ring. My heart ached. I wanted to slip it on my finger and rush into his arms. But, I couldn't, in good conscience, do that without starting the process of full disclosure. "But, before I wear that, I have some things to confess."

He didn't pull away, but I felt him stiffen. He nodded finally. "Okay."

"Okay." I held his hand tighter. Just as I opened my mouth, my phone buzzed on the table. I jumped. "Sorry." I glanced at it. It was a text from Mallory: *Haven't been kidnapped or murdered yet. Having fun. xoxo*

I cleared my throat. "I told Mal to text me every hour. She's on a date." Will nodded. I had to spit this out, he looked worried. "Okay. Where to even start?" With my free hand, I took a generous swallow of wine and then looked Will right in the eyes. *Here goes, my confession for the second time this week.* "I get images from animals who have suffered recent trauma. When I touch them, I get images of the thing that caused them pain or fear. Not just images, sometimes scents or feelings." I pressed my lips together and searched Will's face for a reaction.

He was staring at me without blinking at first. Then soft laughter escaped his throat. Then it faded and he frowned. "You're serious?"

"Yes."

"Oh." He pulled his hand away, the ring receding with it. "I don't really understand. You're telling me you're a psychic?"

He said the word "psychic" with unconcealed distain. I winced, remembering our conversations about psychics and how he thought they were all charlatans. I tamped down my pride and fear with another generous swallow of wine.

"Well, I can't read minds or predict the future. It's only animals that I get images from." Well, I can feel people's emotions sometimes, too, but I needed to keep this simple. *One freak confession at a time.* "I don't know why. Maybe because they don't have any barriers up or I don't have any barriers up with them. I've just always been able to know when they've been traumatized by something. Do they show me? Or am I just picking up on the images in their mind like a radio signal? I don't know how it works. It just does." I shrugged. "The first time I remember it happening was when I was seven."

Will was staring at me and I couldn't read his expression at all, which was harder than if he would laugh or something. I picked up my knife and spread some spinach dip on bread to give him time to gather his thoughts. I swallowed the whole thing before he responded.

"I don't know what to say. I mean, I have felt like you've been keeping something from me. You don't talk about your family. You seem reluctant to open up. But, I just don't..." He shook his head. "My whole world is based on facts, Darwin. I just have never been able to swallow the whole psychic thing."

I frowned and watched the young couple behind us laughing and whispering intimately to each other. I suddenly would have killed to just be a normal person. But I wasn't. I couldn't change who I was, so Will either had to accept that, or not.

Fear of losing him began to squeeze my chest. The nightmares were coming true. "Okay. So, I'll give you a fact. I didn't just stumble upon that townhouse by accident the night you and Karma found me and saved my life. When I touched Karma after Mad Dog died, I saw that townhouse as clear as if I was standing in front of it. So, I knew that's where to look to find out who killed Mad Dog."

Will's face paled, his lips pressed together and his blue eyes took on a stormy gray tint. "Well, that wasn't very smart."

"No, probably not. But, it's what I had to do. Would you have believed me if I'd come to you and said, 'Hey, you have to stake out this townhouse because I got a vision from the dog?'"

Will made some noise in frustration. "No. But—" his phone buzzed. He pulled it from his pocket and then, swearing under his breath, he answered it with a curt, "Detective Blake." He pinched the bridge of his nose with his eyes closed and then sighed. "All right. Be there in five."

"Duty calls?" I tried to smile but my heart was too heavy.

"I'm sorry. A body's been found." He bowed his head then placed the ring back in the box and took a few bills out of his wallet. He laid them on the table. "That should cover it." Then came over to my side and kneeled down beside me, taking my hand. "We will continue this conversation tomorrow. In the meantime," he put the box in my hand and closed my fingers around it, "hold on to this. I really am sorry." He was already in work mode, I could tell. He kissed the top of my head and was gone.

A kiss on the top of the head? That was it? I sighed. Blinking back tears, I finished off the crab cakes, had another glass of wine and watched the crowds mill about in their groups of friends and family. Everyone seemed to be happy, except me. Well, me and whoever the poor soul was who had Will working tonight.

CHAPTER TWENTY-SIX

Thursday morning started off slower at the boutique than it had been. We figured people were sleeping in after all the Halloween festivities. Sylvia had brought a box of chocolate croissants in. We were gathered around the snack table, listening to Mallory gush about her date with Sammy while we got our sugar buzz on. I hadn't had a chance to talk to Mal about what had happened with Will or show her the ring yet. I had decided, when she'd come in last night happy as a clam, that I didn't want to spoil her mood. I guess I was wrong about Sammy. He did seem to be making my sister happy and was being a gentleman.

Suddenly Frankie burst through the door, wearing a black satin robe and matching slippers, a paper in her hand. Glancing around frantically, she spotted me and rushed over.

"Holy Santa on a Sunday, Darwin! Have you seen the paper?" She thrust it out at me.

"Are you still in your pajamas?" I asked, putting down my croissant. I wiped my fingers and took the paper from her. When I saw the front page, my pulse quickened.

"What is it? Read out loud!" Sylvia said.

I read, trying to wrap my mind around what I was reading. "The body of Alba Balderas was found Halloween night in her car in the parking lot of Beachgate condos." *Beachgate condos?* I glanced up at Frankie then kept going. "She had been bitten numerous times by a Jararaca, a poisonous pit viper, and succumbed to her injuries before she was found. Miss Balderas was a novice snake collector and a box that the deadly pit viper escaped from was found in the back seat of her car. The snake has been taken to St. Pete's Serpentarium where it will be used to educate the public."

I stared at the photo of the parking lot of Beachgate condos at the top of the page. Then looked up at Frankie. "Jararaca... I recognize that name. That was one of the snakes Bernard said he had. This can't be a coincidence."

"Another death from snake bite?" Mallory crossed her arms. "Definitely not."

"Not just that." Frankie had her hands on her ample hips. "That's where Nova Diaz lives. Do you think she had something to do with this poor woman's death?"

"I don't know. Will got called out last night to a body that had been found. I can try to find out something from him. Weird, though, this lady," I glanced back through the article for her name, "Alba Balderas, she wasn't on the list of people with a license to own dangerous snakes, either. I guess that law isn't enforced very well."

"She could have been new to the area, maybe." Frankie swallowed a bite of croissant.

Sylvia licked chocolate off of her French manicure. "See, is what people get for messing with the *Diabo*!"

"The devil?" Mallory asked. When Sylvia nodded emphatically, Mallory rolled her eyes.

I handed the paper back to Frankie. "Well, we can't spy on the devil. But, we can spy on Nova Diaz."

I still had to talk to Jet Jamison, too. I was pretty sure the rattler that bit Rose was the one that supposedly "escaped" from him. The investigation was definitely heating up.

* * *

After we closed up the boutique, I called Zach. He agreed to go with me to Jet Jamison's house. This time, when we knocked on the door, a tall, red-haired guy with a matching red beard answered, wearing just a faded pair of blue jeans.

"Jet Jamison?" I asked.

"Depends on who's asking," he grunted, eyeing Zach warily. I stuck out my hand. "I'm Darwin Winters. This is my friend Zach. We just have a quick question for you about your snakes." I watched his pupils shrink and his jaw tighten. I had already put him on edge. "Won't take but a minute," I assured him.

"Look, I just renewed my license and submitted my inventory records. Since when do y'all make house calls?"

"Oh, we're not... those people. Just civilians."

His eyes narrowed. "What do you want then?" His fist tightened around the door frame.

I glanced back at Zach nervously. He had his hands in his pockets, acting casual, but I could tell he was on edge, also.

"Okay, well, we heard that you recently lost track of a rattlesnake that you had captured." I paused as his face hardened. Normally, I would bail at this point, but I did feel a bit braver with Zach beside me so I continued, "Is this true?"

He stuck his tongue in the side of his cheek. "What business would that be of yours?"

I smiled politely. "My friend Zach here is Rose Faraday's son. That name ring a bell to you?"

His eyes darted to Zach. I saw a drop of sweat run down the side of his face. "Nope." He was lying. And not doing a very good job of it. "Is it supposed to?"

"Rose Faraday was the woman who was bitten in her own condo by a rattlesnake. She died." I crossed my arms. "So, we are just looking for some closure. Trying to figure out why and how the rattlesnake would be hanging around her very occupied housing community. Any ideas?"

Jet Jamison scanned the road behind us, then let his muddy brown eyes move from Zach to me. "You seem like nice folks. Let me give you a little piece of advice that I strongly suggest you follow." He leaned toward me, his voice dropping to a gruff whisper. "Leave it alone."

I was suddenly staring at the door as he shut it in my face. I spun around and looked at Zach. "Did he just threaten us?"

Zach was still staring at the door. The red sparks were glistening in his eyes. "Come on, we got what we needed here."

I followed him back down the driveway. "Will might believe me now and start investigating your mother's death as a murder since I've told him about my visions. He's coming over later tonight. I'll tell him about this conversation, too." *Yeah, and maybe the moon will start bouncing across the bay. Stop it, Darwin. Give the man a chance.*

CHAPTER TWENTY-SEVEN

I came home to a hungry cat, a wrecked living room and a note from Mallory. I pulled the note off the fridge while Lucky stared at me from the bar, complaining. Repeatedly.

"Went to the museum and dinner with Sammy. Be home around 11." I sighed and retrieved Lucky's diet kibble from the cupboard. At least one of us was having a good time.

I went to fill her bowl. Then I noticed she had only eaten the middle out of the kibble. Shaking my head, I got a spoon and mixed them around, just adding a bit of new food. I also fished a hair tie from her water bowl and gave her fresh water. Weird kitty. She hungrily devoured the kibble. Next I went into the living room and picked up Mallory's shoes, guitar and practice candles and carried them up to the guestroom. After filling the dishwasher, sweeping the cat hair off the wood floor, changing the litter box and putting the pillows back on the sofa, I decided to make a large Caesar salad and garlic bread for Will and I to snack on while we had our big discussion. Plus it kept me busy. I needed to keep busy.

I had just pulled the bread out of the oven, cleaned up the kitchen and thrown Lucky's hair tie on the sofa for the millionth time when Will buzzed the gate.

"Show time," I said to Lucky, lifting her off the bar and depositing her on the back of the sofa.

"Hi." Will gave me an awkward hug as I let him in. It was a hug someone would give an injured person, or a mental patient.

His signature coconut smell wafted over me. I blinked back the disappointment and tried to just be happy that he was here at all. "Come on in. I hope you're hungry. I made us a giant Caesar salad with fresh parmesan."

"Sounds great." He followed me into the kitchen and put the white wine he brought on the counter. "Opener?"

"The drawer right by your leg," I answered.

Will nodded at Lucky, still perched on the back of the sofa, her tail flicking violently. "So, you still have Rose Faraday's cat, huh?"

"For now." I sliced up the still warm bread and arranged it on a platter. "Mallory will probably take her back home to Savannah when she leaves. They've gotten pretty attached to each other." I carried the bread basket to the smoked glass dining table.

Will followed with the two glasses of wine. "How long is she staying?"

"That's the question of the month." I surveyed the table. *What was missing?* I had already put out some large wooden bowls, forks, napkins, freshly ground pepper. Ah, some water glasses. "She's made a friend here so I don't think she's interested in leaving anytime soon. Go on, dig in. I'll just get us some water."

Will took a seat and dished out the salad to both of our bowls. "A guy friend, I take it?"

"Yep. Sammy Harris. You know him?" I sat down.

"Yes. He's pretty well known in St. Pete. Pilots for the rich." Will said, glancing at me sideways. "He's got some interesting friends."

"Seems like a nice guy." I shrugged. "Though the whole snake thing he and his friends are into is kind of creepy." I broke off a piece of bread. "Speaking of... was that poor woman that died of a snake bite last night the one you got called away for? Alba something?" When he glanced up at me, I shrugged. "It was in the paper this morning."

His face darkened. A strong wave of anger emanated from him. It caught me off guard. I'd never felt anger from him before. He stabbed into his salad with a vengeance. "Alba Balderas. She shouldn't have died. Very suspicious. I think your paranoia may be rubbing off on me." He looked up, giving me a soft smile.

I wanted to point out to him that I'm not paranoid but I stuffed my mouth with salad instead and let him talk.

"To the public it looks like a cut and dry case of an amateur snake collector not taking the necessary precautions, right? She was transporting the snake, didn't secure the container, it got out and bit her. Case closed." He shook his head. "But the thing is, she wasn't an amateur snake collector."

"What was she?" I asked, taking a sip of wine.

He stared at me and I could tell he was struggling with his answer. Finally his chin dropped. "I can't say yet." He reached over and squeezed my hand. "I promise, though, I'll tell you everything about this case when it's closed. It's a strange one."

"Okay." We ate in silence for a moment and then I couldn't help myself. "Hey, there's a woman who lives in those condos who's in pretty tight with the local snake collectors. In fact, she's Bernard Grayson's girlfriend. Her name is Nova Diaz. You might want to check her out."

Will suddenly started choking and coughing, grabbing for his water. I jumped up and patted his back. "Are you okay? Will? Say something!" I had heard someone with a blocked airway wouldn't be able to speak so you should make sure they can talk to you.

He held up his hand and squeaked out an, "I'm okay." I sat back down warily as he cleared his throat. He didn't look okay. His eyes were watering. His face was blotchy. He took a deep breath, stared at me and then drained his wine glass. Then stared at me again.

I was starting to feel like I did something wrong. "Will? What's wrong?"

He stood up, retrieved the wine bottle, filled his glass and topped mine off. My stomach was beginning to knot up. I played with a piece of lettuce in my bowl. "Did I do something wrong?"

He took a long swig from his glass and then turned in the chair so he was facing me. "No. You just... surprised me, Darwin. How did you know her?"

"Nova Diaz?" He nodded. "I met her at Bernard Grayson's house the night I went to the Masquerade Ball with Zach. Though, she seemed off somehow. There are some things about her that don't add up." Should I tell him about the gun? Or about her threatening me and Zach?

His brows furrowed. "Listen, I've been thinking about this whole psychic thing with you and I have a theory. I think that you are just hyper observant. You know, like you unconsciously pick up on all these clues about people and it feels like a sixth sense."

My heart sank. He really couldn't accept the truth about me. "Right. A sixth sense based on observed facts." Facts were king in his world. It wasn't his fault, really. He'd held a certain belief all his life about psychics. I couldn't expect him to change that belief overnight. Just for me. "You're probably right." Better he thought this about me than think I was a freak. Only I was a freak. So I was back to hiding who I am from him.

"Hey." He reached out and took both my hands. "You look like I just ran over your dog. I'm trying to understand, Darwin. I mean, this is a compliment. Detectives would kill to have your observational abilities. What you picked up about... Nova Diaz, that's spot on."

I was busy trying to keep the tears at bay so I couldn't respond. Which made Will feel like he needed to keep trying to make me feel better. Which was just making me feel worse.

"Okay, I'm going to share some information with you that I shouldn't. You cannot let it this leave the room. Promise?"

I nodded half-heartedly. "Sure. Promise."

"Okay. You were right about Nova Diaz. She was hiding something. That wasn't her real name. Her real name was Alba Balderas." He paused and let that sink in.

"Alba? But," I gasped, "then it was Nova... I mean, the woman I knew as Nova... who was bitten and died?"

"Yes."

"Holy..." It was my turn to take a large swig of wine. I thought about the last time I saw Nova... er, Alba, sitting there cleaning her gun in her sundress. *She was dead?* Oh, heavens. Well, I could take her off the suspect list. Small comfort. "This can't be a coincidence, Will." I shook my head. "A second snake bite victim in St. Pete in a month?"

I wondered how Bernard had taken the news. He must be devastated. No matter how shady the guy may be, he was definitely smitten with her. I couldn't imagine him being involved in her death. Did someone who had access to his snake house steal a Jararaca from him? Or were they trying to frame him by using the same type of poisonous snake he owned?

"There's something else," Will said. "She wasn't just a snake collector. She was a special agent with the U.S. fish and wildlife service."

"What?!" You could have knocked me out of my chair with a feather. My mind was reeling with the implications of this news. "Why?" Well, that would explain her having a gun. *So, she was one of the good guys?* Her warning to be careful wasn't a threat at all, then. She really was telling me and Zach to be careful. My head was spinning. "Why was she using a different name?"

"She was working undercover. Her meeting Bernard Grayson was a set-up from the beginning to investigate an anonymous tip Fish and Wildlife received about him, and some illegal reptile dealings. They got a search warrant for Grayson's home last night but found nothing. All his snakes were legal and properly labeled and chipped." He shook his head. "You see why I know she didn't just get careless with securing the container? Something is fishy here. There's no evidence. Short of a taped confession, I don't know how we're going to prove someone besides the snake was responsible for her death." He smiled wryly at me. "And that wasn't a challenge for you to get involved in this."

I knew he was only trying to lighten the mood, but I was already involved. He just refused to accept why. "So, how did Bernard take the news that his girlfriend was an undercover agent?"

"Apparently he was devastated and very cooperative."

I thought about how happy he seemed with her. I couldn't believe she was gone. So sad. "When I was at his house, he told me he had one of those snakes, the Jararaca."

Will nodded. "Okay, I'll check the reports from last night and see if that snake was still accounted for."

"There's another person you might want to talk to. His name's Jet Jamison. He apparently caught a few wild rattlesnakes and one supposedly got loose right before Rose Faraday was killed."

"Where did you get that information?"

"From Sammy Harris. I was trying to figure out how the rattler that bit Rose was so close to a neighborhood. Then I talked to Jet Jamison and he wouldn't confirm or deny having a rattler get loose. Just kind of threatened us to leave it alone."

Will sighed. "Us?"

I cringed inwardly. "Me and Zach."

"You're not very good at leaving the investigating to the investigators, are you?"

Ouch. "Well, no one was investigating Rose's death and Zach deserves to find out what really happened to his mother."

"It was considered an accidental death."

"But now that Nova, I mean, Alba has died the same way, you will investigate Rose's death as murder, right?"

"Can't really interrogate a rattlesnake, Darwin."

He was frustrated. I could see that, but I couldn't tell if it was with the case or me. "But you can interrogate the person who cut the lanai screen and slipped the snake into Rose's condo."

His eyes narrowed. "Did you see something that night you're not telling me about?"

Oh heavens, I did it again. "Yes." I shook my head. "I mean no. Not *see* the way you mean. I told you, I get visions from animals and the night we found Lucky, when I touched her, I saw a person in a black hooded jacket slipping the snake into the lanai." There, full disclosure. What he did with the information was up to him. "Maybe you could check out Jet Jamison's alibi for that night?"

Will ran a hand roughly through his hair and blew out a long sigh. "You know what? I've discussed too much with you already. You shouldn't be involved and..." He pushed his chair back. "I don't know what you want me to say. I mean, if you weren't physically there to see a person in a black jacket by her lanai that night, then it's just fantasy, Darwin. It's not evidence. I can't go accusing people of murder if I don't have real evidence."

I saw him wince when the words came out, instantly regretted them. Still, they stung. I swallowed the lump in my throat and turned away.

I felt his frustration like a desert heat wave. "I'm sorry," he offered. "I shouldn't have said that. I should go."

I stood up with him, carrying our bowls to the kitchen just to have something to do. I felt numb. Lucky stared up at me from the back of the sofa as I passed with a look that bordered on pity. I put the dishes in the sink and then rooted through my straw bag as Will went to the door.

"It's okay." I swiped at a warm tear that had escaped as I approached him. "Better I know now how you feel." I put the ring box in his hand. "It shouldn't be this hard, right?"

He closed his fist around the box, his eyes shut. Mallory came home at that moment. When she saw my face, her smile faded and she moved quietly to the kitchen.

"Darwin..." Will's voice was husky with emotion.

I shook my head. "It's okay. You should go."

His eyes fell to the floor, he nodded and then left.

CHAPTER TWENTY-EIGHT

I stood on the porch where it had all begun. Rose's condo. I had to marvel for a moment at the serendipity of life. If my sister hadn't shown up and decided she wanted to take the ghost tour, we would never have found Lucky. Or, more accurately, she wouldn't have found us. I wouldn't have had the vision of the person in the black jacket slipping the rattlesnake into Rose's lanai, and Rose's death would have been just an unfortunate accident. And the murderer would have forever gone free. A part of me wished that's the way it had happened. But, it didn't. So, here I was.

I shook my head and raised my hand to knock. The door opened before I could touch it. Zach—or more accurately, his tall frame and broad shoulders—took up the bulk of the doorway, his dark hair wet and glistening, like his eyes. His shirt was unbuttoned and a towel was slung over his shoulder.

"Sorry," I stammered, mentally kicking myself for letting my gaze slip down his bare chest to the tattoo across his ribcage: symbols with dark, slashing lines that looked like a word in a foreign language. "Bad time? I can come back."

He stepped back, an amused smile pulling at his mouth. "Never a bad time for you. Come in."

I followed him into the living room, clutching my straw bag close to my body as I took in the condo. The walls had been painted a dark green satin finish; thick burgundy curtains with tassels adorned the windows; a gold chandelier and spun gold tapestry hung heavy in the room. The fireplace mantel held a myriad of photos in ornate frames and various statues, and the place was saturated with the scent of jasmine. Goosebumps formed on my arms. The air conditioner was on full blast, and it was freezing.

As I sat down on the edge of the leather sofa, I noted curiously that it didn't match the rest of the cream velour furniture. Zach tossed aside a satin plum throw pillow and lowered himself onto the loveseat across from me, thankfully buttoning up his shirt.

"So," I began, clearing my throat, "I talked to Will last night and I have some new information for you."

"Go on."

I had thought long and hard on the way over here about whether I should tell Zach about this. After all, I had promised Will this information wouldn't leave my townhouse. But, in the end, this was bigger than me and Will's relationship and bigger than one person's promise. This was about stopping a murderer. I just hoped I could live with the guilt.

I took a deep breath. Now or never. "So, it turns out that Nova Diaz was the woman who died from the snakebite in the Beachside parking lot. Her real name was Alba Balderas and she was an undercover agent for U.S. Fish and Wildlife."

Zach stared at me for a moment as the information sank in. "Really?" He finally shifted in his seat. "U.S. Fish and Wildlife? So, she was investigating Bernard Grayson, I assume?"

I nodded. "Apparently there was an anonymous tip about illegal reptile dealings. But, Will said they searched his place last night and didn't find anything."

"Seems a bit extreme, putting in an undercover agent just because of one anonymous tip." Zach rubbed his hair with the towel. "I didn't even know they had undercover agents."

I stared at the crystal ball on the coffee table. I wondered if Zach used it. "You're right. Will probably just didn't give me the whole story." That thought made me flush. It hadn't occurred to me until that moment. I felt the distance between me and Will expand. I guess he was right in not trusting me with more information. After all, I did just betray his confidence. What kind of person was I turning into? When I glanced up, Zach was staring at me thoughtfully.

"You told Will about your vision of the person slipping the rattler onto the lanai?"

Was I that transparent? I sighed. "Yes."

"And he didn't take it seriously?"

"No. He thinks I'm just hyper observant or something. Oh, and the fact that I wasn't physically there to see the person slip the snake into the lanai, that makes it a fantasy."

"Ouch," Zach said. "Well, he may just need time to process, Darwin. Humans are... well, human. They don't like their beliefs about how the world works shaken up."

I smiled at his attempt to cheer me up. "Thanks. I hope you're right. But, in the meantime, it's up to us to come up with some hard evidence against your mother's and Alba's murderer. Any ideas?"

He stared behind me for a moment. "Well, Bernard is sounding more and more like our guy, especially if he was being investigated by the authorities. And now that he knows he's being investigated, we don't have much time."

"Except for one thing. Bernard wasn't in town the night your mother was murdered. Neither was Sammy. You confirmed that with your contact at the airport, right?"

"Yes." He sighed. "They were in Brazil. Which doesn't leave us much to run with, either."

"Especially because I really think Bernard was in love with Alba. I don't think he'd harm her. Maybe someone killed her to hurt Bernard? Send a message or warning to him?"

Zach nodded. "That's possible. But who?"

"What about Jet Jamison? He actually catches wild rattlesnakes and Sammy said he had one get away. But, what if it didn't get away? What if he just told Sammy that it did?"

"He did seem defensive but what motive would he have? He'd have to really have something against Bernard to resort to murder."

"I don't know. I think we should try to find out what Mr. Jamison was doing the night your mother was killed. If he doesn't have an alibi, then we can work on motive."

"Agreed. Anyone else?"

"Maybe Jack. He had motive, though he doesn't own snakes. I can see if Frankie knows where he was that night."

"Okay. I'll work on Jamison. You work on Jack," Zach said.

I stood to go, sliding my bag on my shoulder. The crystal ball caught my eye again. "That yours?" I nodded toward it.

"My mother's. I haven't had the heart to pack away her things yet."

That surprised me. He must have cared about her on some level he wasn't willing to admit. "Do you scry?"

"No." He shook his head. "Scrying is more about getting information through focus of the conscious mind, allowing the subconscious to present to it knowledge from the Whole. I never learned to do this because I get information from touch." He stood and suddenly we were too close again.

I wanted to ask him what he was, but my need to move away from him was stronger than my curiosity. "Okay." I moved around the other side of the coffee table. "I'll contact you when I find out about Jack."

"Darwin?"

I turned back to him. "Yes?"

"Thank you... for your help. I will repay you one day."

I shook my head. "Not necessary. I'm doing it for Rose."

CHAPTER TWENTY-NINE

Saturday, we were just about to close up when Sammy came through the door with a bouquet of red roses partially covering his face.

"Mal!" I called to her. "Sammy's here."

"Hey." I looked up from rubber-banding the checks together and got a better look at him. "Heavens! What happened to your eye?"

"Oh," he chuckled, putting the roses on the counter, "Jet Jamison was a little sore with me for ratting him out about the rattlesnake getting loose."

My hand flew to my mouth. "I'm so sorry. I didn't know he'd figure out who told us."

"No biggie." He smiled as Mallory came towards him. "He hits like a girl."

"Whoa." Mallory cupped his face. "What happened?"

"Just a little argument. But," he lifted the roses and handed them to her, "don't you worry yourself about such things." He then pulled two tickets out of his pocket. "I have dinner theatre tickets, front and center tonight."

Mallory lifted her nose from the sweet velvety petals. "I do believe you're trying to spoil me." She laughed.

"Trying my best." He kissed her cheek.

She blushed and turned to me. "All right if I don't help you close up tonight?"

"Sure," I said. "Go on. Have fun."

"Thanks, Sis." She gave me a quick hug and then left with Sammy.

I still felt bad that my questioning Jamison had gotten Sammy hurt. Jamison seemed like a pretty violent guy. Maybe we were on the right track with our suspicions of him. I'd call Zach after closing and see if he had found out anything.

Turned out I didn't have to call him. He was waiting for me when I stepped out of the boutique.

"Hi," I said, surprised.

"Jamison has a girlfriend named Sandy. I spoke to her and she said they were supposed to go out the night my mother was killed but Jamison cancelled on her. Said he was sick. She remembered the date because she thought he was cheating on her."

Right to the point, as always. Where did this man get his social skills? Or lack of them was more like it. "Hello, Darwin, how are you? I'm just dandy, Zach, thanks for asking," I teased him.

"Sorry," he said, and actually seemed to mean it.

I waved off his apology. "So Jamison doesn't have an alibi for that night?"

"Doesn't appear to."

"So the next question is, does he have a motive?"

"Or was he hired to kill my mother?"

"Right. That's a possibility. Money's as good a motivation as any," I said. "Well, turns out Frankie went with Jack to Bernard's party, the night your mother was there telling fortunes. She didn't notice anything odd that night. But, the next weekend she didn't see Jack. She said it wasn't unusual for them to not talk for a week or so but still, she couldn't give him an alibi for the night your mother was killed."

"So, they both stay on the suspect list."

"Looks that way." I watched an elderly couple stroll by, their hands entangled. I fought off the thought of Will and the sadness that came with that thought. "So, where do we go from here?"

Zach had his hands resting on his hips. He shrugged. "Dinner?"

"Dinner?" I had planned on going home and eating leftovers, but I didn't feel like being alone tonight. "Sure. Just let me run up and feed Lucky. I'll meet you at Parkshore Grill. Grab an outside table, please."

Zach gave me a small smile and nodded.

At the gate, I glanced back, watching him walk away. Two over-dressed teenage girls, wearing too much makeup and stiletto heels, also turned to watch him as he passed. Their appreciative giggling trailed behind them down the sidewalk.

When had I let my guard down with him? He was dangerous, I was sure of it. But, he was now my partner in a way that Will wasn't. That made me sad and confused.

* * *

Zach cut into a rare steak. "My contact at the airport said Bernard left for Brazil early Friday morning, just got back in early this evening. I find his frequent trips there suspicious. Especially right on the heels of being investigated." He slid the chunk of meat off his fork with his teeth and chewed slowly.

"It does seem a bit suspect that he goes that often." I noticed Zach glancing at me. It felt like he wanted to say something but wasn't sure how I'd react. I chewed and swallowed a bite of salad. "Does your contact know why he goes to Brazil so often? He can't be buying snakes every time."

"No." His voice dropped. He put down his fork and met my eyes. "But he does know which hangar Bernard's private plane is in. He said there are always two thuggish-looking guys standing outside the hangar when Bernard returns. Like they're guarding something." He folded his hands on the table and leaned toward me, his voice dropping. "He gave me the code to get in the gate."

I put down my fork and stared at him. "You want to sneak into the hangar and check out his plane?"

"Don't you? There has to be something important about their trips and about what they're bringing back to need bodyguards."

I thought about it. No, I really didn't want to. It was trespassing. And illegal. We could end up in jail or worse. And the last time I decided to trespass, when I checked out the townhouse, it hadn't turned out so well.

I groaned and rubbed the space between my brows. I could feel the tension pulsing there as I tried to keep the memory of the townhouse at bay. But this time, I wasn't alone. And something had to give.

If we could find out what Bernard was up to, maybe we could figure out if he had enough motive to kill Rose. If not, we could at least cross him off the suspect list. I dropped my hands and met his gaze. "Okay. When?"

His eyes blazed and then hardened. "Finish your dinner. Then we'll take a walk."

I nodded, although I wasn't sure I could swallow another bite. I suddenly felt vulnerable. It was a new feeling. *Who am I to be doing this? I'm just a girl from Savannah.* I stared across the park lawn to the bay water, without really seeing it. *Isn't that what I'm trying to be? Just a girl?* I had denied my heritage to be normal and suddenly it felt all wrong, like I had stripped off my armor and laid down my sword, but I was going to go into battle anyway. I shook off the thought, tucking it in the back of my mind to sort out later.

When I looked up, Zach was very still, watching me.

I leaned back, away from him. "You're not trying to read my mind, are you? Because that would kinda cross a personal boundary."

He frowned. "I don't have to. Your eyes betray your thoughts... and your struggle."

I felt my face grow hot. "I've only got one thought right now. To figure out who murdered your mother and Alba Diaz, before someone else dies." I pushed my plate away and put on some false bravado. "Ready when you are."

CHAPTER THIRTY

Albert Whitted Airport had a single guard that we could see. One lone security truck sitting unoccupied in front of the airport administration office. One man cruised the area, checking to make sure everything was secure.

We took our time walking along 8th Avenue. Darkness had fallen and the air was cool. A slight breeze held the scents of salt and fuel. After we left the restaurant, I had gone up and changed into yoga pants, a t-shirt, light jacket and sneakers in case we had to do any running. Odds of that seemed pretty high.

My heart was pounding in my chest. I glanced at Zach. His jaw was clenched. Determined. Focused. Like a panther, yellow eyes gleaming. I decided I wouldn't want to run into him in the dark, and I was glad he was on my side.

The small airport stretched out on our left as a series of tan hangars behind a chain linked fence. Private planes sat parked behind them like large, silent birds waiting to be airborne. The tower lights blinked in the distance. It seemed ominously quiet for a working airport.

Zach motioned to me with a sideways jerk of his head, and I followed him through a small parking lot to a security box in front of a gate. He punched a code in the keypad. The creak of the gate startled me as it rolled open. This was it. No turning back.

We tried to act casual as we walked onto the airport grounds, but I could feel the tension speeding up our steps.

"We're looking for hanger number eleven," Zach whispered. "Should be on the end over here."

I struggled to keep up with him without breaking into a jog. My breathing was shallow. Heavens, we hadn't even talked about how we were going to get in.

Then we suddenly stopped as we both saw 'Hanger 11' painted on the side of one of the buildings. I glanced up at Zach. *Now what?*

"Come on." He pushed forward.

The large rolling shutter doors were clamped down tight. We jogged around to the back of the hangar. There was an office door. Zach pulled something out of his pocket and slipped it into the lock.

I grabbed his arm. "What if there's an alarm set?"

His eyes glistened in the dark. "Then we're screwed."

I heard a click and held my breath as he pushed the door open. We both stood still for a second, listening. No alarm. Thank heavens. We slipped inside, shutting the door behind us.

I couldn't believe it. We were in!

I glanced around the dark office. It was mostly bare. One small wooden desk with a few papers scattered on it, a rolling desk chair, and a file cabinet squatting in the corner. Zach crossed the small room in a few steps, pulling open the desk drawers. I went to the file cabinet and tried to do the same, but it was locked.

I suddenly got a bad feeling and second thoughts. "Zach?"

"Yeah?"

"What are we doing here? I mean, short of a recorded confession, there's no way to pin your mother's and Alba's death on Bernard even if he is the murderer."

Zach stood, thinking for a moment. Then nodding, his expression hardened. "Come on."

I sighed and followed him out of the office and into the hangar, wishing I would have thought to leave Mallory a note, letting her know where I was. Just in case.

A single jet occupied the hangar. It was long and sleek with a row of oval windows. The building frame was a web of steel scaffolding above us; the walls were sheets of metal. A few skylights above allowed in enough moonlight for us to see we were alone. The air filled my lungs, warm and stifling. I peeled off my jacket and tied it around my waist.

A low whistling sound escaped Zach as we approached the plane. "This baby's a Gulfstream G650, the fastest and longest range business jet in the world. No wonder they didn't have any problem flying back and forth to Brazil for the weekend." He frowned. "Bernard Grayson's a lot richer than I thought. A lot richer than one man should be."

We walked around the front, beneath the jet to the other side. The stairs had been left in the down position. I stepped up onto them and climbed each one silently, listening for any movement in the plane. Zach followed close behind. I could feel the heat radiating off him, warming my back.

I stepped into the bowels of the cabin and glanced around. Clusters of cream colored chairs lined the wall on the right, glossy tables between them. A flat screen TV sat on a large matching counter space to the left. The cabin smelled like leather and money.

I moved deeper into the cabin. Zach suddenly grabbed my arm. His mouth pressed into my hair. "Shhh. I think I heard movement."

I turned my head slightly to look up at him. He nodded to the curtain at the back of the jet. *Was somebody back there?* Slipping around me, he stepped in front to take the lead.

I scanned the cabin frantically for something to use as a weapon. Nothing. I stared at Zach's wide shoulders and muscular build. Surely, he could fight if he needed to? My breathing sounded too loud in my own ears. The more I tried to quiet it, the harder it was to breathe.

Oh heavens, I was beginning to hyperventilate. Sweat trickled between my shoulder blades. Something had to give or I was going to pass out. Closing my eyes, I sought out the surrounding bay waters. I was too rusty to control it. But I could use the comfort of its presence to control my fear. Make the anxiety manageable.

Feeling better, I opened my eyes and took a shuddering breath. Zach had reached the curtain. Pulling it gently to one side, he peered in. One, two heartbeats. He motioned back to me and slid it open wide enough for us to enter. I pushed forward. This part was a living area, complete with a cream colored sofa, coffee table, a wall full of kitchen equipment—microwave, coffee pot, sink. Zach pointed to another set of thick, blue curtains further back into the jet. I nodded.

He moved cautiously around the coffee table. I wasn't so cautious and smacked my knee hard. Stifling a scream, I limped behind him. His large hand gripped the curtain and he stuck his head beyond it. My heart threatened to knock right through my chest as he slid it open. I peered around him. A bedroom? My face flushed as I realized my chest was pressed up against Zach. I backed up, putting a few inches between us.

Two steps lead up to an octagon shaped bed. A sea-blue satin bedspread covered the bed. On top of it sat wooden boxes. Inside the boxes, something was moving, bumping against the walls.

"I'll give you three guesses what's in those boxes," Zach said warily.

"I only need one," I answered. "But why would they leave them in the jet?"

Suddenly we heard the horrifying sound of the hanger doors rolling open. We looked at each other, eyes wide.

Zach's jaw tightened. "To come back for them under the cover of night."

I glanced around. We were trapped. Zach pulled me up the two steps and closed the curtain behind us. We sat on the satin bedspread. The tiny bedroom morphed into a sauna.

Voices and laughter reverberated outside in the hangar.

"We can't stay in here." I motioned to the boxes on the bed behind us. "Not if they came back for those."

"You're right," Zach said. He grabbed my hand and led us back out into the living area. We glanced around frantically. "All right. Here's the plan." He turned and looked down at me. His dark eyes glowed with pinpricks of red. "You hide in the bathroom. I'm going to confront Bernard."

"What?" I shook my head. "No! You can't do that."

"I have to. This may be our only chance to get to the bottom of all this. To get to the truth."

"But if Bernard is the murderer, he's not going to just confess and let you go."

"That's a chance I'm willing to take." He rested a large palm against my damp cheek. "But I can't let you take that chance, Darwin."

"Oh no you don't." I pushed his hand away. "We're in this together. Let's go."

In hindsight, this may have been one of those times when I should have swallowed my pride.

CHAPTER THIRTY-ONE

The surprise on Bernard's face was priceless as we appeared in the jet doorway. In any other situation, I would have appreciated the ability to surprise the bugger out of someone. Like maybe an actual surprise party.

"Hi," I said, waving.

"Jesus! What the..." He yanked the cigar from his mouth, eyes wide.

Three burly men acted immediately, reaching us in a few strides, pulling us out of the jet's cabin and down the short flight of stairs. I recognized one of them as the scar-faced guy who let us into Bernard's party.

"Hey!" I tried to pull my arm free. "You're hurting me." This apparently was thug code for "please squeeze my arm tighter".

"Well, well, well." Bernard's body stiffened as he moved his icy gaze from Zach to me. "What do we have here? Snoops." He turned to one of his guys. "Shut the door."

My mouth went dry as the guy obeyed the order. The hanger door rolled shut with a definitive boom. Scarface held Zach by the arm and pulled a gun from his waistband. My mind raced. *All this violence for snakes? Why?*

"You caught us red-handed," Zach said. His voice was steady and calm. His hands were clasped in front of him. "No need to get jumpy. We'll wait for the police without giving you any trouble."

"The police?" Bernard shoved one hand in the pocket of his slacks and puffed on his cigar. A mean little smile played on his mouth. He nodded to Scarface.

"Kneel," the guy grunted, pushing Zach to his knees. The guy had one hand on Zach's shoulder and the gun in the other.

"We have no need for the police. We have our own methods of dealing with trespassers."

Thug number three emerged from the plane with zip ties. Panic and anger battled within me. Anger won.

"Your own methods? Like using a poisonous snake to murder Rose Faraday and Alba Diaz?" Out of the corner of my eye, I saw Zach shaking his head, trying to stop me. But, it was too late. This was our moment to find out the truth about who murdered Rose and Alba. "All for what? Some illegal snakes?" I had no idea what Bernard's motive might be but we had come too far not to find out.

Bernard's face turned crimson. He lowered his head and stood like that for a moment. I snuck a glance sideways. Zach was sliding his hands into his pants pockets. I hoped he had a miracle in there.

Finally, Bernard lifted his head and glared at me. I shrank back. His eyes held both rage and pity.

"Little girl, you have just sealed your own fate." He nodded again at Scarface.

Quick as a flash, the thug raised his arm and hit Zach in the temple with the butt of the gun. I screamed and broke free as Zach collapsed in a heap. A strong hand grabbed my hair before I could reach him. My scalp caught fire. My knees buckled. I stifled another scream as he forced me to kneel. Choking back a sob, I winced as the guy pulled the zip ties tight on me, binding my hands and feet. I glanced sideways. Zach was out cold. The guy then worked to bind Zach's hands and feet. In case he woke up I supposed. This wasn't the plan at all. Okay, so there was no plan. But, if there was, this definitely wouldn't be it.

Bernard ambled over to us. Gray cigar smoke curled around him and floated toward my face as he kneeled in front of me. My throat burned. I coughed until my eyes watered. "Why? Why did you kill them?" I managed to choke out.

"Why?" he chuckled. He ran his tongue along his top teeth as he considered me. Then he stood and crushed his cigar under his shoe. "You are a brave girl, so before you die, I will tell you what you want to know. My gift to you."

Die? Well, thanks for the heads up. "A gift card would've been fine," I said, adrenalin making me tremble as I watched Bernard disappear into the jet.

When he returned and knelt in front of me again, I scrambled back, pushing into the legs of the thug standing behind me.

"No, no," Bernard cooed, holding the snake with both hands. It curled its tail around his forearm. "This one is not poisonous."

I eyed the snake suspiciously. It was a brilliant orange with a pattern of black circles. Beady eyes were set high in its striped head. A tongue flicked the air obsessively but the rest of the snake was not very active. Then I noticed a bulge a few inches up from its tail. *Ewe.* It must be digesting one of those frozen rats.

I remembered what he collected. "A Brazilian rainbow boa?"

"No. A mule." A raspy laugh escaped him. The men chuckled with him.

I didn't get the joke. "I don't get it? These snakes aren't illegal." I had a sudden glimmer of hope that we hadn't stumbled into them doing anything wrong and they would let us go. Maybe they were just trying to scare us. That hope, however, died a quick death with Bernard's next words.

"No. They are not." His eyes caught mine. "But the diamonds inside of them are."

CHAPTER THIRTY-TWO

I stared at the bulge in the snake, stunned. "Diamonds?" I croaked.

"Yes." He caressed the snake, its scales glittering in the moonlight. "These beauties help us bring the diamonds mined from the Cinta Larga Indian reservation in Brazil to the U.S."

I stared at the bulge in the snake's body and shuddered. I didn't even want to think about how they got the diamonds in there. No wonder that poor boa had a stomachache. "Stolen diamonds?"

"No, of course not," Bernard said, seemingly agitated by the accusation that he was a thief. "We buy them. But, mining in the Indian reservation is illegal, so the diamonds are sold on the black market and we pay a fraction of what they're worth."

He seemed very proud of himself. My stomach churned. "But what does this have to do with Rose Faraday? Why kill her?"

"Ah." His lips thinned. "It was unfortunate that she was such a talented psychic. When she did my reading, she saw the Indian reservation and the diamonds. I couldn't let her repeat that to anyone, even if she hadn't put it together."

"So you slipped the rattlesnake into her condo?"

"Well, no." He took a deep breath. "I didn't have a rattler on hand so I traded a few diamonds for the job and made sure I was out of town when it happened."

"Jet Jamison?" I asked.

Bernard glanced up at me and stopped stroking the snake. "Yes. My, you have been a busy girl."

Not as busy as you. "And that's why you invited Zach to your party? To see if his mother had mentioned the Indian reservation or diamonds to him?"

"Yes." He glanced over at Zach. "Too bad he didn't leave well enough alone. Seemed like a nice guy."

I didn't like the way he used past tense in reference to Zach. "Then you killed Alba because you found out she was an undercover agent?"

Crinkles appeared between his brows and his eyes clouded. "Yes. That one. She broke my heart. I bought a six carat diamond just for her. I was going to propose." His face hardened. "Stupid mistake." He stood abruptly. "No more loose ends. Take them to the office."

"Ouch!" I squealed as the thug pulled me up by my arms. Then the wind was knocked out of me as he threw me over his shoulder, carried me across the hangar and dumped me on the office floor with a thud. My tailbone screamed from the assault. "Not very nice," I said, trying to catch my breath.

He shook his head and moved out of the way as the other two thugs dropped Zach's still unconscious body beside me, shutting the door on their way out. Well, at least they didn't shoot us. Yet.

"Zach," I whispered, wriggling over and nudging him with my shoulder. "Zach, please wake up!" My mind raced. I glanced frantically around. One door, one window. No way I could open either with my hands and feet bound.

Suddenly, I heard the low rumbling sound of the doors rolling open again. *Were they leaving? Oh, please let them be leaving.*

One of the thugs burst back into the room and shoved a rag into my mouth, tying it roughly with a piece of nylon rope. "Be quiet," he hissed. He did the same to Zach and then quickly exited the room.

Voices were right outside the door but I couldn't make out any words. Claustrophobia began to set in. I could only suck in the stale air through my nose. I squeezed my eyes shut and tried to calm my labored breathing, reaching out with my mind to the water. As my mind and body calmed, my eyes flew open.

Mallory. I sensed Mallory! She went out with Sammy tonight. He must have brought her here.

No!

I tried to scream, but the rag was doing its job. I nudged Zach harder. No response. I looked around wildly. Okay. I had to calm down and think. I worked on taking deep breaths. In. Out. In. Out.

I closed my eyes and immediately sensed water in a close proximity. Someone had brought water with them into the hangar.

Moving into the space in my consciousness that was able to connect to the water, I concentrated, losing all sense of time, willing the water to move.

I opened my eyes as the voices escalated. I was spent, my energy depleted from the effort. *How much time had passed? And had it worked?*

There was shouting. A scream and then silence.

Precious seconds ticked by. *What's happening? Mallory!* And then the door opened and my baby sister was there. Eyes wild, hands and feet bound, being dumped on the floor next to me.

"Darwin!" She cried, fear and tears stinging her eyes. "What's going on?" The thug shoved a rag in her mouth, too.

I felt so helpless at that moment. So terrified. It welled up inside me like a tidal wave with nowhere to go. The pressure in my skull was almost unbearable. By moving the water in the water bottle, I had just meant to alert Mallory I was there, so she could get help. I should have known she would react immediately, without thinking it through. Now she was in danger, too.

Sammy pushed the thug out of the doorway and stared at Mallory, running a hand through his hair, his face pale. "Mallory, I'm so sorry," he said finally. "I didn't know they would be here." He turned from the room and shouting ensued. Sammy and Bernard barked at each other, their voices escalating. I scooted next to Mallory and tried to comfort her, pressing my shoulder against hers.

"I'm getting her out of here!" Sammy yelled.

He tried to come back into the office, but Scarface pulled his gun and leveled it at him. Sammy stopped dead. His eyes moved helplessly to Mallory before the thug backed him out of the doorway and slammed the door.

Mallory and I stared at each other, both of our chests rising and falling rapidly. I knew they weren't going to let us go. We knew too much.

Zach moaned and stirred.

Zach! I scooted back across the floor and nudged him with my knees. I screamed through the cloth and then decided it wasn't worth the expended energy. Twisting so I could use my feet to try and wake him, I pushed at his body, rocking him back and forth. His head rolled to the side and he coughed into the rag.

My heart knocked against my chest as the door opened.

There stood Bernard, holding one of the wooden boxes. Scarface entered behind him.

Then it hit me. Of course, he wouldn't shoot us. Guns weren't his weapon of choice. My heart raced. Time was up. We had no plan. No one knew we were here. Was this really it? Was he really going to get away with murder again?

Strolling over to the desk, he sat the box down and looked us over, a new cigar held in his teeth. There was a thump and thud against the box walls. I felt Mallory go still beside me.

Bernard removed the cigar and smiled down at us. "Want to hear my favorite proverb, ladies?" He continued as if we did. "Unless a serpent devours a serpent it will not become a dragon. Which, translated means unless one power absorbs another, it will not become great." His eyes cooled to blue ice. "People fear snakes. But they have a very useful job in the food chain. They eradicate pests."

As he turned away from us, a flash of fire burst in his hand. He jumped and then cursing, stomped hard on his cigar, grinding it into the cement floor.

I glanced at Mallory. Her eyes were glowing green with fury. I was impressed with how much she had grown in her magick. She'd never been able to control it while she was angry before.

Bernard whirled back, eyeing us, and then nodded at Scarface, who stood with his arms crossed against the wall. "Release the Jararaca."

Oh, heavens! Jararaca? The pit viper that killed Alba? I pushed myself against the wall and pulled my knees up against my body. Scarface gave the box a mean shake, smiling at us. Then he opened the box and, not one, but two grayish-brown snakes reared their heads. I heard Mallory whimper. She scooted slowly over to press her body against mine. She was trembling. Scarface left the office with a salute, closing the door definitively behind him.

I blinked back the tears and blinding panic. *Think, Darwin.* I kept my body still, non-threatening, hoping Mallory would do the same. It was hard to think through the sound of the blood pounding in my own ears. I could still sense the water out in the hangar. I could kick myself for not practicing. Maybe if I could calm down and concentrate, I could still use it somehow.

The box tipped over as the thick, muscular bodies slid out onto the desk. A ripple moved through their entire length as they flicked their tongues toward us. The longer one slid off the desk and landed with a soft thud on the concrete floor.

I felt Mallory's fear. Dark waves washed over me. The snakes were visibly agitated. The smaller one slithered under the desk. *Great.* Not knowing where it was seemed worse.

Zach shifted beside me. Oh heavens. *Be still, Zach!*

Zach moaned. I ripped my gaze from the snake to him. His eyes fluttered open and he blinked, staring at me. I could see the confusion. I shook my head and moved my gaze back to the snake, hoping he would look there, also.

Unfortunately, he slid his bound feet over to see what I was looking at. The pit viper jerked at the movement. His head lifted higher into the air. Agitated and nervous. Not a good state.

Zach slowly sat up, his eyes trained on the snake. I could hear the long, slow breathes he was taking through his nose.

I caught movement to my right. The second snake peered out from beneath the desk. Its tongue flicked the air in front of us. It inched its way out, sliding toward us.

Zach slowly looked at me. I stared back into the depths of his dark eyes. He glanced purposefully at Mallory and then back at me. He was trying to tell me something. My eyes narrowed. *What? What are you planning?*

One single nod. And then he kicked at the snake, lashing out at it with his feet, simultaneously lunging sideways to throw his body as a human shield over us both.

The wind was knocked out of me. I heard Mallory's muffled scream beside me.

CHAPTER THIRTY-THREE

The Jararacas struck simultaneously. Quick as a whip, they sunk their fangs into Zach and then disappeared beneath the desk. I looked down in horror at the blood beginning to seep from two holes in his leg and two holes in his neck.

He needed medical attention immediately. I couldn't sit here and watch him suffer the same fate as his mother and Alba. We had to get out of here and get him to a hospital, but how? Obviously, Bernard's plan was to let us die. How long would he leave us in here? All night? Until we had all succumbed to bites? Anger was now replacing panic.

I looked down at Zach. His eyes were focused on Mallory. He kept darting his eyes from her to the bite wound on his leg and back.

Suddenly, I saw Mallory's eyes widen in surprise. She leaned across me, studying the blood running down Zach's neck. Her head jerked back. Then she nodded at him.

Struggling, he lifted himself off of us as carefully as he could. I winced as his weight pinned my legs to the ground briefly. Then felt relief as he succeeded in sitting up.

I glanced from Zach to Mallory. Something was going on. I knew the venom inside him was a ticking time bomb, probably already clotting his blood. His mother had a heart attack from one bite from a poisonous snake. I hoped to heaven his heart was healthy.

Mallory closed her eyes and leaned her head back against the wall. I felt her emotions level, her fear subside. Heard her breathing calm. She was concentrating. It was almost as if...

Wait. What in the world? I stared at the wound in Zach's neck. His blood glowed a fluorescent red. It flowed from the holes like hot lava. What kind of blood glows? My eyes jerked up to his face. He was staring at the door.

Suddenly, I watched in awe as four perfect drops of his blood lifted from his skin. I leaned away as they circled and merged into a single ball in the air. My own skin tingled. The hair stood up on my arms.

I glanced at Mallory. Her eyes were squeezed closed in concentration and suddenly I understood—not the how, but the why of—what was happening. She had found a source of fire in Zach's blood. How was that even possible?

What in heaven's name was he?

I shook off the question. It could wait until we got out of here. If we got out of here.

Zach and I both watched as the ball of his blood pulsed and expanded. The feeling of being close to an energy source intensified. A high buzzing noise filled the room. Tiny roots of white light formed within the center of the ball, expanding it further.

It reached the size of a basketball and then shot forward, splintering the door. A few seconds ticked by. Then BOOM!

An explosion rocked the steel hangar. I felt it vibrate in my bones. I pressed closer to Mallory to shield her. After a few more long seconds, smoke began to seep in through the hole in the door.

I sensed water. A lot of it. The hangar had a sprinkler system! I realized I was shaking. It stopped as my whole being felt quenched.

I rolled my head toward Mallory. The smattering of freckles stood out on her pale skin. Her lashes were wet. I had never been more proud of her. Mallory had saved our lives. I leaned forward and touched my forehead to my little sister's, letting the tears of relief fall.

Sirens grew in the distance, coming closer. I lifted my head and looked at Zach. He turned to meet my stare. He didn't seem to be in any pain. Again, the question surfaced. *What was he?*

Within moments, the sirens were right outside the hangar. I wondered if Bernard had gotten hurt in the explosion or if he had gotten away. I was angry he was still going to get away with murdering Rose and Alba. But at least I could tell the police about his illegal diamond business. He would answer for something.

A figure appeared behind the smoke in the doorway, peering into the office.

"What the... Darwin!"

Will burst through the damaged door. Two uniformed officers followed right behind him. He surveyed the scene as he knelt down and gently removed the gag from my mouth. The two officers did the same for Mallory and Zach.

"Darwin. Jesus..." His hands stroked my hair and he lifted my face. "Are you hurt?"

I smiled up into his sky blue eyes, feeling his emotions wash over me. They were so intense, I felt giddy. My smile widened. "No. But, Will?"

"Yes?"

"There are two pit vipers loose under the desk."

CHAPTER THIRTY-FOUR

I stood by the back of the ambulance, a blanket wrapped around my shoulders. Mallory lay on the stretcher inside. A paramedic was taking her blood pressure. I knew she'd be fine. She was just exhausted from expending so much energy. She needed rest and sunlight.

Red lights swirled on the buildings around us. Fire trucks and squad cars crowded the space around the hangar. Smoke still hung in the night air.

I watched Will rub his forehead as two officers spoke to him. He looked around and we made eye contact. Another officer approached him and, after a brief conversation, he nodded and made his way over to me.

"Hi," he said, standing in front of me in his slacks and tie, a badge clipped to his belt. The worry pinching his face made me melt. "They didn't hurt you?"

"No." I tilted my chin to look up at him. He was so close. I wanted to just fall against his chest. I wanted his arms around me. But, we weren't there anymore. I wasn't sure where we were. "I'm not hurt." Not on the outside, anyway. "What about Bernard and Sammy? Was anyone hurt in the explosion?" I knew Mallory wasn't trying to hurt anyone and she would be horrified if she had.

"Grayson and the others have been taken to the hospital with second degree burns. They'll live. The sprinkler system did its job quickly." Pulling out a notebook he said, "I'm going to need you to tell me everything that happened here tonight."

"Everything? Are you sure?" I looked up into his eyes. "I think it will be more than you want to know."

He turned and stared at the plane still smoking in the hangar. Then he looked back at me and took a deep breath. He gazed into my eyes, questions rising and then subsiding. Suddenly looking tired, he shook his head. "Okay, just tell me the events I can put in my report."

I pulled the blanket tighter around me, realizing I had a question for him first. "Wait, how did you get here so fast, anyway?"

He shrugged. "We were already on our way here when we saw the explosion." He stopped. "I shouldn't tell you..." then he blew out a deep breath. "Oh, why the hell not? After the undercover agent was killed, a woman came forward and alerted us to Grayson's illegal diamond business. She's a vet and Grayson had been blackmailing her into removing the condoms full of diamonds from the snakes once he brought them to the states. He threatened her kids. Told her he could get to them at any time. She's a single mother and was terrified of him. But after the agent turned up dead, she knew she had to do something."

"Dr. Brown?" I asked.

"Yes." Will nodded.

Well, that explained why her demeanor changed when I asked her about a sick snake. I remembered the two cute little girls in her photos. Poor woman, I couldn't blame her for wanting to protect them. I'm glad she did the right thing in the end though.

"So, we were on our way to arrest him." Relief softened his mouth as he smiled at me. "Luckily for you three. I had no idea you were in there." He must have seen my disappointment. "What's wrong?"

My heart sank and the frustration returned. "Well, if you already knew about the illegal diamond business, then we didn't find out anything to help you. Bernard confessed to me that he killed Rose and Alba using the poisonous snakes, but we still have no proof of that. So, he gets away with murder anyway."

"No. He doesn't." Zach walked up to us.

I glanced at his neck. No swelling. No redness. No evidence of the bite at all. He had completely healed.

He held out his cell phone between us. My voice came out of it when he clicked play.

"Then you killed Alba because you found out she was an undercover agent?"

Bernard's voice answered. *"Yes. That one. She broke my heart. I bought a six carat diamond just for her. I was going to propose. Stupid mistake."* A brief pause and then, *"No more loose ends. Take them to the office."*

He clicked it off and handed it to Will. Will took it, blinking in disbelief.

"You recorded our conversation? But h... how?" I stammered, trying to think back to when he could have done it. "You were knocked out cold."

"I started the recording before I was hit. You said we needed a taped confession. I was counting on the fact that you like to ask questions."

My mouth opened and closed like a fish out of water. I wasn't sure whether to be insulted or flattered.

Will was still staring at Zach. "A recorded murder confession from Bernard Grayson?" He made a choking sound. "I don't know what to say."

Zach smiled, though his eyes were hard black marbles. "You're welcome." He glanced at me, still addressing Will. "Take care of her." He walked away, leaving us standing there.

Will's face suddenly broke out in a grin and then he stared at the ground, hands resting loosely on his hips. I watched as a myriad of emotions rolled over him. Finally, he looked back up at me. "I don't like the fact that you put yourself in danger... again, but this is..." He couldn't find the word. He cleared his throat. "We have a lot to talk about, Darwin."

I nodded, feeling sad and tired suddenly. Talking to me would be a good start. Believing me would be even better.

CHAPTER THIRTY-FIVE

I tucked a blanket around Mallory and brought her some tea. It was late, almost midnight, by the time we got home. Neither one of us wanted to be alone so we were camped out in the living room. I pulled my feet up underneath me on the loveseat, my hair still damp from the shower, and stared at my little sister. *What would I have done if she hadn't been there? If Father hadn't visited her and told her I would need her? Or if she had been shunning her gift like I had?* The thought was too unbearable to hold in my mind for long.

My eyes were beginning to feel like lead when Lucky suddenly raised her head from behind Mallory's knees. I watched curiously as she craned her neck and focused her stare on the patio doors. I scanned the floor for the usual suspect—some kind of bug. Nothing. Lucky hopped up onto Mallory's hip, a pink hair tie clenched in her small jaws. She perched there, her ears twitching madly.

"What is it, girl?" I whispered. Did she see something out on the patio? It was so dark out there but cats did have better night vision than us. *Oh heavens, let it not be a snake!*

Suddenly, Lucky leaped silently to the floor. I gasped. "Mallory!"

Mallory blinked, still groggy. "What?"

"Look!" I pointed to Lucky as she padded across the floor for the first time since we had found her.

Mallory rubbed her eyes and pushed herself up slowly on one elbow. "What is she doing?"

"Don't know," I whispered. As we watched, Lucky dropped the hair tie and tilted her chin up, still focused on something above her. She let out a happy chirp and began purring like a motorboat, then flopped down onto her side and stretched out, pink paws and claws reaching and stretching to both corners of the room. The purring grew louder. *What did she see? Or who?*

Mallory and I looked at each other.

"Do you smell jasmine?" I whispered.

"Yeah." Mallory nodded. "Definitely jasmine."

The moment was too big to put into words so we just shared a smile.

* * *

Two days later I was hugging my sister as her suitcase and guitar were being loaded into the back of a cab.

"I'm sorry it turned out Sammy knew about the diamond smuggling, Mal."

"Yeah," she sighed, "me too. Live and learn, I guess." She shook her head. "I still can't believe Bernard Grayson had that poor woman killed over being a gifted psychic. Maybe you're right about hiding who we are from people."

I took her hand. "No, don't you change now. You saved our lives because you refused to be ashamed of your gift. Father would have been proud of you. Or is proud of you." It was all so confusing. I smiled and wiped a tear from her flushed cheek. "Are you sure you don't want to stay longer?" I held onto her hand.

She squeezed my hand and sighed. She still looked tired. Her normally bright eyes were dull and sunken. "I need to go home." Then in a dramatic voice, she added, "My work here is done."

"And what fine work it was." I shook my head, still in disbelief of how everything turned out. "Bernard Grayson will be going away for a long time."

"After he recovers from being caught in the explosion." She frowned. "Oh, I almost forgot. I talked to Grandma Winters this morning and told her about our... adventure." She glanced around and then leaned closer to me. "She told me to tell you to stay away from Zach Faraday. Said it sounds like he's part jinn and they are dangerous."

I stared at her. "Jinn? As in Genie?"

"Yep."

"Well, that explains a lot." I hadn't heard from Zach since that night. I wasn't sure how I felt about that. If I was honest, a little disappointed.

She lifted the cat carrier. "All right. Say goodbye to Lady Luck."

I leaned over and stuck my finger into the carrier, scratching under Lucky's silky chin. "Good work, Lucky. You helped us catch your mom's killer. You enjoy your new home now and take care of Mallory." Lucky's big green eyes stared at me. She mewed. I laughed. "I'll miss you, too."

Mallory and I hugged tightly one more time. Before she slid into the backseat, she turned to me. "Grandma Winters also said to tell you to practice. That way your little sister won't have to fly here and save your butt again." She grinned and then disappeared into the cab.

I crossed my arms as I watched the taxi drive her away. She was right. With our magick came accountability. I had no right to deny the gift our father had given us. It was dangerous. And selfish.

"Hey."

I whirled around. Will stood behind me, his hands shoved into his jean's pockets. His dark hair was mussed and he looked like he hadn't slept in days. He looked younger and more vulnerable than I had ever seen him.

My heart leapt into my throat. "Hey, what are you doing here?"

"I wanted to take you to lunch." He flashed that little half smile that melted my heart. "And talk. Unofficially."

I gave the taxi one more glance as it turned the corner and disappeared out of sight. "All right." We walked down to Parkshore Grill. I wanted to slip my hand in his but he kept them in his pockets. Besides, I had no right to be thinking that way. I had no idea where we stood.

"So your sister went home?"

"Yeah. She took Lucky back to Savannah. Funny how things work out. I'll actually miss them both.

That big old townhouse is going to seem awfully empty now."

I took a seat at an available table, expecting Will to slide in across from me. Instead, he knelt on the sidewalk in front of me.

"Will?" I eyed him questioningly.

He took my hand and lifted his eyes to meet mine. "Darwin Winters, I promise to keep an open mind and try my best to put aside my doubts and prejudices." He pulled the amethyst ring from his pocket and held it next to my ring finger. "Can you forgive me for being such a jerk?"

I laughed. Tears stung my eyes. "Oh, Will, I never thought that."

He slipped the ring on my finger and pressed his warm mouth to my hand. "I mean it, Darwin. This is my solemn commitment to you."

A family walking by clapped and smiled at us. I stared at the ring, speechless, then pulled him up and wrapped my arms around his neck, burying my face in his shoulder. Heavens it felt good to be in his arms again.

He pulled away and lifted my chin so we were eye to eye. "And I need you to promise that you'll stop putting yourself in dangerous situations."

I blinked innocently at him. "Why Detective Blake, whatever are you talking about?"

He gave me a hard look. "I mean it, Darwin. You're shortening my life span."

I laughed. "Well, I wouldn't want that on my conscience." I held my hand over my heart, the hand now sporting a promise ring from this beautiful creature kneeling before me. I felt like the luckiest gal in the world. "I promise that I will try my best not to put myself in dangerous situations."

His eyes narrowed. "Why don't I believe you?"

I opened my mouth in mock surprise. "Doubting me already?"

He stood and kissed my mouth softly. I melted into him. Better this way. I didn't have to explain to him that I don't put myself in these situations. The animals get me involved. And how could I say no to them?